# THE CAPTAIN

Point Loma

By Cam Séamus

©2022

First Edition: 2022

ISBN 978-1-7362349-2-1

Library of Congress Catalog Number 2022910866

Developmental Editor - Dave Bone
Senior Editor - Morgan Bone
Editor - Laurie Taylor
Editor– Kimberly Albury
Cover Design – Andy Carpenter Design

To learn more about the author and his other projects, visit:

https://cutwaterpublishing.com

# Contents

To my friends on the docks who took me in like a stray dog –

I am eternally grateful to you all.

# Point Loma

# Point Loma

## I

The captain's face had worn experience, wisdom, and failure; all were gained while crossing oceans. At the present moment it wore only experience, and Captain Jack Kelly had no intention of adding failure to his countenance - not today, never again.

A sudden shift of the wind as it gusted, laid the sailboat hard over. The guests reached for something to hold on to in their fight against gravity, while the captain resisted the boat's intrinsic inclination to round up into the wind. He held the huge stainless-steel wheel to the right as he fought the pressure on the helm of *Zentimental*.

The sailboat was only a few years old, built in the typical flatter bottom style of newer European sailboats. The topsides of the hull were painted a deep navy color, and she flew a long streamer off the backstay advertising the charter company. He often referred to her as, "a beautiful lady that deserves his attention."

*Zentimental* was not his, yet he felt a deep connection with this boat. In much the same way a race car driver speaks to the racing machine, Jack spoke to the boat, "OK," he said quietly, "let's have some fun."

He kept his strong, suntanned hands firmly on the helm, digging her chines harder into the blue-green water inside of Point Loma. His smile gave the charter guests comfort as the boat heeled over further. Jack's experience told him that it was about to happen again.

The captain shouted above the noise of the wind, "Hold on to something!"

The sunglasses they wore couldn't conceal the range of emotion on their faces which displayed delight, concern, and fear.

Jack saw all of it simultaneously: the wind on the water, the rocky shore of Point Loma, the sail trim, his course, and their faces. Rays of light glistened off the helm and filtered through his sunglasses as he took a deep breath of cool, salty, ocean air. He looked up and watched as pelicans and seagulls circled nearby, diving to catch the small fish that sustained them. The image in his mind was like a painted canvas with the cliffs towering above the sea. He deliberately captured it so he could recall it at night, when he was alone, when he fought against the darkness. Captain Jack Kelly took none of it for granted. He had learned how quickly the sea could impose lasting change. The cost of this lesson had been too steep, and it was a cost he could never bear again.

Jack looked up at the majestic peninsula towering above and visualized the wind accelerating toward them. It was as if the long finger of land had directed the wind toward his sailboat. As if the finger was pointing at him, warning him, and reminding him. The predictable sea breezes in San Diego were mostly northwest, except where the finger bent them towards unsuspecting vessels. The captain had felt the first shift, and he knew that the second and possibly third were just ahead of him as he approached the harbor entrance.

Twice a day, Jack made this trip in and out of San Diego Harbor and now, it was as natural to him as breathing. He had fought hard to overcome obstacles and earn his place behind the helm. In many ways, he was still fighting. He fought to be free of his past, and the voice inside which reminded him of his failure.

Without conscious thought, the captain made a slight course correction in anticipation of the next bend in the wind as the peninsula reminded everyone of its presence. Ballast Point lay a little over a mile ahead as he picked his line on the outside of the marked channel. He smiled as he watched two unsuspecting sailboats in front of him as they were rounded up into the wind by its sudden force, their helms losing the ability to hold the boats on course as bows turned directly into the wind, taking the pressure off the sails.

"Sit down and hang on everyone, it's about to get a bit sporty!" the captain shouted with enthusiasm.

These changes were of little concern for the captain, or for the guests who listened to his briefing, "One hand for the boat, one hand for yourself." Not all passengers heeded the admonishment; one man was too arrogant and had taken too many pulls from a flask. It was foolish to disregard the multidimensional movement of a ten-ton sailboat.

Jack loved being a captain on most days, but as he watched today's footloose guest, his frustration and anxiety built. He thought, *Doesn't this guy know I can lose my license if something happens, and I'm found guilty of over-serving?* Jack also realized that even if this man had known, he would not have cared. The man's deep disregard for others had been on display since the moment he boarded. It wouldn't matter to a Coast Guard inquiry that Jack had not actually poured the drinks; he was the one who was in command when it happened. He knew that they would not be sympathetic if he stood before another review board - *especially to him.*

When the final gust hit the sailboat, it was hard, sudden, and without warning. The drunk man, who had neither listened nor complied, was standing insolently in the cockpit even after the captain had told him to sit down. But this was a man who gave orders, not took them. When the captain gave the order, he merely smirked and shook his head. There was no time for him to reconsider.

The abrupt tilt and simultaneous turning of the boat caused the inebriated man to completely lose his balance as he toppled over. He fell forward onto the brightly varnished tabletop bolted to the cockpit floor, and his head was the first thing to hit the corner of the table. The forceful impact split the sunburned skin of his forehead wide open, knocking him unconscious.

Most of the passengers let out screams and yelps as they watched the man's blood run from his head, staining the teak decks. The two who didn't scream responded in ways that could not have been more unlike. The youngest pulled out his phone and started filming, saying, "This is sick!" The other was a middle-aged woman who quickly crossed over to the man and knelt down beside him. After the initial shock, other phones came out and began filming, posting, and texting.

The captain released his firm grip on the wheel and the boat followed the instructions of her designer, rounding up gently into the wind. He eased the sheets on the main and genoa sails and let the boat go into irons with its sails flapping noisily and aimlessly.

Grabbing the first aid kit beneath the helm seat, the captain pulled on a pair of surgical gloves and walked toward the unconscious man. The woman who knelt beside him said, "I'm an ER nurse" in an authoritative tone. He passed the kit and a pair of gloves to her. Without another word, she pulled on the gloves, popped the metal release latches, lifted the lid, took out a gauze pad and began to apply light pressure on the bleeding wound. One of the other guests helped her get him onto his back, between the table and the cockpit seat. The captain handed her a flotation cushion to put under his head and walked back to the helm. He picked up the VHF radio mic and said the words he had only said once before, "Mayday, Mayday, Mayday," the phrase that mariners use only when there is immediate threat to the vessel, or when someone needs immediate medical assistance. The word "Mayday" haunted this captain more than any other in the English lexicon. To Jack, it could only mean failure, pain, loss, and death. His training took over and allowed him to do the job at hand while he fought the release of long pent-up emotions.

Immediately after the Mayday, he continued, "This is sailing vessel *Zentimental*, we are located just inside Point Loma, due west…" Jack paused for a second as he glanced over his right shoulder to confirm what he knew without his eyes seeing it. "We are approximately one-hundred yards west of San Diego channel marker Green 7, I repeat one-hundred yards due west of San Diego channel marker Green 7, how copy?"

He released the mic and waited for what seemed like minutes. The radio crackled back to life a few seconds later.

"Vessel calling Mayday, this is Coast Guard Sector San Diego, is there an immediate threat to the vessel or is there someone on board requiring urgent medical attention?"

Jack knew that San Diego Bay pleasure boaters were often unaware of its dangers. The narrow bay, with its large presence of U.S. Navy, Coast Guard, Homeland Security, and Harbor Police, could lull you into a false sense of security. The captains heard the emergency calls on a regular basis: a boat on fire, someone suffered a heart attack, a boat capsized; the list went on. Even though it was a small bay, being on the water was still dangerous; that was a lesson Jack had learned and would never forget.

"Coast Guard Sector San Diego, this is *Zentimental*, the boat is in no danger, we have an unconscious, unresponsive male, approximately forty-five years old with a head injury, request you dispatch assistance, over."

"Good copy *Zentimental*, you are requesting medical assistance… stand by…" The radio went silent. Then, "All boats in your immediate area are dispatched to other emergencies – are you able to proceed into dock?"

The captain sighed, his mind flashed to another hearing board, or worse - another dead passenger. Jack couldn't believe this was happening again. *I never should have applied to have my license reinstated*, he thought in the brief seconds before his response.

Even though they were only about three miles to the entrance of America's Cup Harbor where they had departed, a sailboat, even under diesel power, could take thirty minutes to get there, and the ebbing tide would further impede their movement toward the harbor.

Then he keyed the mic in his hand, raising it close to his lips, "Good Copy Sector San Diego – no immediate assistance available." The captain paused while intentionally holding the mic key down to block the response while he thought for a second. Then he said, "Request permission to put in at Coast Guard Pier at Ballast Point and have an EMT meet us there."

Jack glanced up and looked into the eye of a low-flying pelican who stared back at him, completely unaware of his problems. Time seemed to slow to a standstill as he gazed into the seabird's eye and waited for the Coast Guard's response.

The earnest young voice came back on the radio, "Roger *Zentimental*, requesting to put in at Ballast Point. Stand By."

VHF channel 16, the international emergency channel, remained quiet as did the boat, and many other mariners in the area. They all listened intently for the response of the Coast Guard. Unbeknownst to Jack, there were nearby vessels ready to alter their course if needed, to lend assistance.

While they waited for the Coast Guard's response, Jack was plying his trade as a sailboat captain, muscle memory more than conscious thought driving his actions. He began by furling the headsail and firing up the diesel engine. Then, turning the boat back toward the narrow channel opening at Ballast Point, he began to motor sail into the harbor. With the angle of the wind clocking to the north, and the outgoing tide, the captain knew this was his best option. A few minutes later, the radio came alive.

"*Zentimental*, this is Coast Guard Sector San Diego, permission to drop your medical passenger off at Ballast Point is granted. Repeat, permission is granted. How copy?"

The captain quickly tied the roller furling line to the cleat and picked up the mic, "Good copy Coast Guard, *Zentimental* standing by on one-six – our AIS is on if Ballast Point wants to watch our approach."

"Roger *Zentimental*, we see you on AIS. Coast Guard standing by on one-six and two-two alpha."

*Sail this Bay* charter company required the Automatic Identification Scheme device known as AIS, to be turned on at all times, so they could locate a boat in need of assistance.

While the sailboat moved toward the entrance of the harbor, the nurse continued to monitor the passenger who was still unconscious. As *Zentimental* approached Ballast Point, the captain picked up his mic again, "Hailing Coast Guard Ballast Point, Coast Guard Ballast Point, Coast Guard Ballast Point, this is sailing vessel *Zentimental*."

The reply came quickly, "Go ahead *Zentimental*."

"Did you let Navy Security for Point Loma Submarine Base know that I was coming? Don't want them getting an itchy trigger finger."

The Navy had patrol boats with machine guns on station outside the water fence that surrounded the small base.

Jack waited for the response.

"Roger *Zentimental*, they are expecting you."

"I'm passing Ballast Point now – right in front of your window, I'll drop my main and come on in."

"We have line handlers waiting on the docks for you, and the medical team is standing by to assist. Coast Guard standing by on one-six, and two-two Alpha."

"Roger that Coast Guard. *Zentimental* standing by on channel sixteen."

## II

The old bar sat overhanging the water, supported by pilings driven deep into the muddy bottom of the bay. The smell in the room was a strange potpourri of old wood, a well-used grill, partially clean bar, and musky men with hints of salt, fish, and diesel. Somehow it all worked together in a way that few found offensive. Those who did find it offensive would probably also be offended by the nature of the conversation they would overhear. This crowd did not care about political correctness, or the latest 'woke' rules.

The walls were covered in ship half-hull hand carvings that if sold at auction might have been worth more than the business itself. The bar was less than half full, normal for a weekday. Women and men displayed the deep tan colors in their faces and exposed sections of skin. Most wore uniforms, only in the sense that the shirt or hat had a logo of the company that wrote the checks which paid for their beers. There was the steady hum from the low murmur of quiet conversation, punctured by a roar from the group when a point was scored in the game on the TV. It was a hall of fellowship, celebration, and commiseration for the working captains at the west end of the bay. Tourists were tolerated, because many had sailed with those captains. They were not necessarily welcomed, unless of course they were buying. This was a captain's hall, and it was their time to speak freely with those that understood.

"It was a hell of a day, Bradley," Captain Jack said to one of his peers as he pulled his stool closer to the bar and took a long pull on the Hazy IPA which dusted his upper lip with foam.

Jack began to tell his friend of the day's events.

"Jesus," said the other captain, "It's days like this you'd rather be a cab driver!"

"There's drunk assholes in those too," said Jack.

The two captains grinned and chuckled.

Only those in this small fraternity really understood the nuance of the work. Most of the time it was pure joy. They knew how lucky they were to be paid to sail a boat in paradise. But like all professions, it had downsides: cleaning up puke, listening to know-it-alls for three hours at a crack, no tips after pouring your energy out, and some long, cold days. But the good days outweighed the bad, and the bad were worked out over beers.

Bradley raised his glass and offered a toast, "Here's to drunk assholes – may they be anywhere but on our boats!"

A few of the other captains at the bar heard the toast and joined in, "Cheers!" their chorus rang out.

"Was the guy OK?" Bradley asked with genuine concern.

Jack nodded as he replied, "Mostly just dealing with a hangover compounded by a concussion – he'll live. I'm pissed, too; I think he was already drunk when they boarded him."

Bradley was nodding in agreement as he took another drink of his beer, and then chimed in, "It's a problem. The dock managers check, but sometimes they slip through. If something happens out there, it's our license on the line."

A captain's license was not easily obtained, but it could be easily lost. The ones held by Jack and Bradley required over seven-hundred days on the water outside of the harbor and a battery of testing. It was a long and expensive journey. At the end they were given a small book, like that of a passport, which contained the license that allowed them to take passengers out for hire. They assumed command of the vessel and the responsibility for the lives of crew and passengers. Either of them could have earned more working in corporate America, but Jack had never met a captain who said he was in it for the money.

Jack nodded and took another sip as the men sat quietly at the bar and contemplated the conversation. He caught the eye of the bartender and glanced toward the two nearly empty glasses that sat on the bar in front of them. The bartender smiled and nodded as the silent transaction took place between the two men.

Jack and Bradley were wholly uninterested in the game on the televisions which hung all over the bar. Bradley looked down at his phone, while Jack looked up at the nautical history on the walls surrounding him.

San Diego had been home to so many ships and the commerce that accompanied them. He wondered what would come after their time had gone. Would the walls someday display pictures of them in front of a bridal party on a sailboat?

"Doubtful," Jack said under his breath.

Jack looked at Bradley and managed a smile as he watched him run his hand through his short, once black hair, now mostly gray. The saltwater had a way of working like a hair spray. As Bradley finished, his hair looked fashionably messy. Jack noticed that his shorts were still unwrinkled and his shirt neatly tucked in. Bradley was the fashionable captain in the group, while the others around him appeared more unkempt and pushed the boundaries of the company's dress code. Bradley was in his mid-fifties, the oldest of the group and he stayed very fit riding his bike almost everywhere. His firm jaw tensed as he read something on his phone screen. The age revealed by his hair color had done nothing to lessen the playfulness of his youth. Jack admired him.

"You should be working the superyachts, Bradley - you sure look the part."

"Too many temptations, Jack."

Both men smiled and turned back toward their beers. Jack looked up at the walls again. There was a tribute to the San Salvador, Cabrillo's ship that sailed to San Diego in the 1500's carrying the first Europeans to see the great West Coast of North America. There were lithographs on the wall of a whaling fleet anchored inside Ballast Point, long before it housed U.S. Navy hunter-killer submarines. As he followed the chronology, he saw massive piles of dead tuna lying motionless awaiting their processing, completing the journey from majestic fish to canned food for people that couldn't fish. There were random pictures of men in high waisted swimsuits from the fifties and sixties, standing proudly next to a trophy catch hanging from the scales at the Big Reel Club. Then, an aerial view of Shelter Island; a place that echoed a time when bigger fish swam in the waters off Southern California.

Bradley broke into Jack's contemplation, "Tip?" he asked.

The captain laughed, "Funny thing, I thought for sure the group would stiff me after the incident."

Bradley cocked his head and said, "Aaand," in a very drawn out and dramatic fashion.

"I think they must have felt guilty that I had to deal with the guy."

The captain paused for dramatic effect. He knew this delay in his answer was playfully annoying Bradley.

"AAAND," Bradley said louder, drawn out, and with greater emphasis, indicating he would have no more of this.

"Three hundred," the captain said as he smiled ear to ear.

"Son of a beautiful bitch," said Bradley. "That's a good day!"

He raised his glass again toward Jack, "Well, does that mean you're buying?"

"Damn right Bradley – bottoms up!"

The fresh beers appeared from the master of the bar, who set them in front of the two sailing captains. Their actual title was not Captain, it was Master, the rank conferred upon them by the U.S. Coast Guard. Master seems like a strange word in the modern day, along with all of its inglorious historical context. But its origins stemmed from the days when the adventurous and brave transited vast oceans on wooden ships, whose captains were literally "master and commander."

Jack was the first to break the silence as they concentrated on the fresh beers.

"I dropped the guy at Ballast Point Coast Guard, and they took him to the hospital – glad he's OK, but what an idiot."

They both glanced up at the game on the big screen above the bar. Bradley knew that the day's events released a wellspring of emotions in his friend; he was one of the very few people that knew the intimate details of Jack's life before San Diego.

"I heard the Mayday, but I wasn't close enough to offer any help. That must have been tough for you."

"Yep," Jack replied.

Bradley didn't want to pry, but he felt like he owed his friend at least a shot at getting it off his chest.

"Was that the first one since…" Bradley started and found himself unable to say her name.

"Yeah."

"You handling it OK?"

"Mostly, it's just hard - a lot of memories, ya know?"

The captain's eye teared a little, and Bradley put a hand on his shoulder.

"I don't know if that will ever go away completely, Jack; that feeling inside you right now."

Captain Jack looked at his friend, "I suppose you're right. I just don't know how to keep going, Brad. It's like an anchor that pulls me down. Ironically, the only thing that distracts me much is running these boats. I can't seem to shake it when I'm not completely occupied with something else. Do you ever feel like that?"

Bradley had indeed felt like that before. He had suffered his own losses, seen his life torn to shreds, and carefully rebuilt it more than once. He knew what it meant to look in the mirror and question everything he'd done in his life. His empathy was forged in pain, his wisdom in experience. Long before he learned to navigate on the ocean, he had learned to navigate in a world where some people hated him only because of his attraction to other men. He knew what it felt like to suffer for a long period of time. Brad also knew when it was time to stop talking about feelings - both for Jack's sake and his own.

"Screw it. How would you feel about getting drunk and stumbling back to our boats?" Bradley offered.

"Bradley, I thought you'd never ask – let's hit Tahiti Tom's, tropical always cheers me up."

The captains drained their beers and Jack paid the bartender.

The cool air on their faces was a refreshing change from the stuffiness of the bar, and they began the short walk to the eastern end of Shelter Island, where the restaurant stood like a monument from the middle of the last century; it was a favorite spot for pictures with its beautiful Polynesian architecture.

"Once in a while I run into a charter guest that doesn't like Tahiti Tom's." Jack said as they strolled down the sidewalk.

Bradley looked at him quizzically, "Who doesn't like Polynesian art and Mai Tais?"

Jack shook his head and sighed, "Some people are just wired wrong."

The captains walked along the quiet street, past the boat yards where boats waited impatiently 'on the hard' for their turn to be painted and repaired. Despite the fact that the island was home to several large resorts, by sunset it was a ghost town. The smell of the marina on the dry winter air began to creep into his nostrils as they walked down the street toward the end of Shelter Island. They talked about things of importance to captains: annoying guests, tips, problems with the charter fleet, and most importantly, projects on their own boats. These were all welcome distractions for Jack.

Once inside the restaurant, the conversation turned completely away from the day's events. Bradley began a long dissertation about the latest boat design elements.

"I don't care what the rating is, I don't want to sail a boat with a bolted-on keel across an ocean!" Bradley hit his fist on the table hard enough to startle the couple next to them.

"I understand. I feel the same way too. It's an unsettling thought a thousand miles offshore."

Bradley continued his rant, "Call me old-fashioned, I still like a full, encapsulated keel."

"How about I just call you old?" Jack smiled at his friend.

"Boy, I'm feelin' it some days, Jack. Especially the damp mornings."

"You hear about Julie's new guy?" asked Bradley.

"That's two this season - good for her," replied Jack.

Then they bounced back and forth about what needed to be fixed on the company boats, plans for sailing trips and other vacations, and generally any topic that would not require the men to contemplate or feel anything of a personal nature.

The very strong Mai Tais were accompanied by coconut shrimp and short ribs. The two men ate and drank and began to feel free as the rum numbed their senses. The room around them ebbed and flowed as patrons waited at the bar, soon to be whisked away to their dining tables. The buzz of activity allowed their normally hyper-focused minds to mercifully wander.

Before Bradley could order a third round, Jack broke in on his attempt to flag down the server, "I think that's it for me, Brad - I'm numb and done."

"It's probably for the best, old man - we're not kids who can bounce back so quickly!" said Bradley, with a slight slur.

Jack settled their bill, and the two men made their way back out into the night. The dim glow of the lights casted eerie shadows on the water, while a few overnight fishing tour vessels made their way out of the harbor. As they walked outside, they passed the tiki, who was known as "Mr. Tom," and gave him a pat for better fortune to come their way. With lighter pockets and lighter hearts, the two captains walked back to their boats.

When they arrived at the gate of Bradley's marina, Jack put a hand on his shoulder as he turned to look at him directly, "You're a good friend, Captain."

They called each other captain occasionally, as a way to convey respect or appreciation.

Bradley smiled at him, "Sleep it off, Jack — tomorrow's another day."

# III

The two men parted for the evening and Jack made his way down to his own boat. He should have taken Bradley's advice and just gone to sleep. But the pull was irresistible; the pain and the darkness inside of him, undeniable. Instead of sleeping off the night's libations, he pulled out a box of photos and a bottle of rum. The Mayday had stirred up too much, and the captain hadn't yet poured enough alcohol down his throat that night to bury the memories - if that was even possible.

Jack took each picture out of the box in the same, deliberate manner, almost like he was performing a religious ritual. It was precise. He looked at a few pictures, poured himself some rum, then took out a few more, then drank more rum. Once he looked at them, they were placed face down on the table, carefully, and tenderly.

Occasionally, the ritual was interrupted as he broke down sobbing. When he was finally done punishing himself, he was too drunk to relocate, falling asleep where he sat, slumped over in a crumpled ball that mirrored his soul; disfigured and nearly lifeless.

The box came out less and less as time wore on, but each time it was the same, and too much rum was always consumed.

# IV

Bradley cried when he returned to his boat. First, he cried for his friend, then he cried for himself. He cried because he wished he could've just been himself all those years, mourning what he had lost while pretending to be someone he was not.

When his tears were dry, he cracked another beer. He thought about Jack's journey to Point Loma in contrast to his own, and he remembered the pain of rebuilding his own life. It seemed that for both himself and Jack, running sailboats was more than a job; it was their tether to life, keeping them loosely bound to sanity. It was a life that he would let no one tear away from him, a life he wouldn't let himself destroy. He knew these things about his life, and he knew that they mattered equally to Jack, even if Jack didn't yet realize it. He resolved that he would stay by his friend's side until Jack regained his perspective, and Bradley didn't care how long it might take.

He lifted his beer and said to the thought of Jack, "I won't let you down my friend."

# V

As the morning light crept into the saloon of his sailboat, the captain's eyes wearily cracked open. He struggled to unstick his tongue from the top of his mouth. Once it was dislodged, he mumbled, "What was I thinking?"

He uncoiled his contorted body and shot a glance at the pile of photographs and half empty bottle of his best rum.

"Christ," he said as he looked at the amount of rum remaining in what had been a nearly full bottle, "How was that even possible?"

He started to count the drinks from The Pilot House to Tahiti Tom's, and then his own private reserve, giving up as he mumbled, "Too damn many."

He pulled himself out of the dining settee, holding on to the rails designed to provide support during storms at sea, now serving to keep him upright. Jack slowly made his way to the refrigerator. Looking outside he cursed the sun as it slammed into his bloodshot eyes.

"It's grey nearly every morning here, why is it so damn bright today?"

A flock of what had once been domestic parrots made prehistoric shrieks outside. It was a sound that he normally enjoyed over a cup of coffee; today it painfully echoed in his head like thunder.

"Shut up!" he screamed out the hatch.

The birds were unaffected by his outburst.

Jack reached into the top loading refrigerator and pulled out a bottle of sparkling water. He held the bottle against the side of his face, letting the cool, moist glass bring relief as he contemplated the need to throw up. He reached for a cup and poured the water into it. Taking both the cup and the bottle with him, he went back to the settee. He desperately wanted to pour a drink, but that wasn't an option because he had charters today. As the cool sparkling water refreshed the desert in his mouth, his stomach started to settle down a bit.

Glancing down at the photos for only a few moments, he was thankful that his bloodshot eyes couldn't focus as he carefully placed them back in the box. The dehydration in his body extended to his eyes, but there was just enough water left to produce a few salty tears as he looked at the two of them together on the boat.

"Pull it together, Jack," he said sternly to himself.

There was an annoying ding from his phone, a reminder that his first sail was at noon. Jack grabbed a heavy canvas boat bag embroidered with his boat's name, *Windborne*. He tossed into it his shaving kit, shorts, polo shirt, and towel. Shirtless and wearing only a sarong he'd picked up in the Marquesas, he slid his feet into flip flops, grabbed the marina key card, and made his way up to the showers.

It was a Tuesday morning, and it was as quiet as it had been the night before. The morning stillness was only interrupted by the occasional jogger as Jack walked along the waterfront to the marina facilities. The parrots had finished their terrorizing wake-up call which had shattered his dehydrated brain. He had drunk the entire bottle of sparkling water along with two aspirin he had chewed and swallowed as his first line of defense against the hangover.

The water was hot enough to create a steam room in the tiled shower. Standing in surrender under the stream, letting his skin soak In the moisture, he pictured the water washing away all of the pain in his body and his soul. From the shower head it washed over him and then disappeared down the drain. He wondered, *Why is water always seen as a symbol of purification?* He leaned the weight of his body against the wall of the shower and stretched his back. *If it is so all-powerful, why can't it erase these stains from my own soul?*

The dark that had haunted him after the accident seemed at times to fade, only to reappear forcefully and without warning, as if it wanted to block out any light in his life, like an evil entity actively engaged in his destruction. He didn't believe in God, ghosts, or goblins, but there were days and nights when he wondered if this darkness had a name. In the dimly lit, steamy shower stall, he was suddenly grateful that the sun was out today. He needed the sun desperately. Perhaps, if only for the afternoon, it would keep the darkness away from his mind.

Running charters had the advantage of distracting a captain - even one in the midst of tragedy. The captain was an entertainer on a stage, in turn acting as a bartender, a tour guide, and above all, the master of the vessel. He regaled his charter guests with jokes and stories of the sea, while being hypervigilant for their safety, and always mindful of other vessels or hazards. A charter captain didn't really have time to reflect on his own problems, which was, in Jack's experience, why some chose to be captains. It was certainly why he chose to continue working as one after his license was reinstated.

He finished the shower and decided that a greasy breakfast was in order to complete his hangover rehabilitation. After a brief stop back on *Windborne* to drop off his shower kit and pick up his briefcase, he began the short walk down to *Point Loma Eggz*. He knew what he would order before walking in the door. It was the same each time - Fishing Boat Captain's Breakfast. It was a pile of six eggs, six pieces of bacon or sausage, hash browns, biscuits, and corned beef, topped with house made gravy. Jack thought it was best to get the eggs over easy, so that the yolks would act as a binder and coagulant for all other ingredients. This was often the subject of serious debate in the restaurant or on the docks, if the topic of breakfast came up. Some argued that hard, crispy eggs had the advantage of adding yet another layer of fried texture, while some preferred scrambled eggs mixed in small bits to create a sort of skillet stew – all of these preferences were worthy of serious consideration. Once, and only once, a new captain had suggested cold, hard-boiled eggs. He received an avalanche of insults and admonishments to keep his "FNG" opinions to himself. This had scared him enough to remain silent in these debates for the rest of the charter season, for he had not yet earned the right to have an opinion.

The food was soon in front of him, and he went to work on it in a deliberate manner. The grease began to work its magic, along with the hot coffee, which the server kept at "high tide." Jack was slowly coming back to life.

One of his friends, Caleb, walked in and caught his eye. He ran an eighty-foot, sport fishing boat out of America's Cup Harbor, just a few hundred yards from where Jack sailed. He was about fifteen years his junior, but they had developed a fast friendship when Jack had first arrived in San Diego. Caleb had introduced Jack to everyone that mattered, and because of those introductions, Jack had found himself in the office of *Sail this Bay.*

"Hey Jack," Caleb began, and before Jack could respond, he smiled and said, "You look like shit."

Jack shook his head in disbelief and said, "Captain, how can you say that to a man who is so clearly standing on death's doorstep?"

They both laughed as Caleb pulled out a chair and sat down. Jack motioned and said sarcastically, "Please Caleb, sit down and join me."

Which is exactly what Caleb had done without the invitation he knew he didn't need.

"So, what happened to you, old man?"

"Oh, nothing much. The Pilot House, Tahiti Tom's, and *Windborne's* provision room."

Caleb laughed in response and said, "Let me guess, IPA, Mai Tai, and rum."

Jack shook his head in a circle to indicate the pain and confusion that his choices had inflicted.

"Are you off today?" Caleb asked in response.

"No," uttered Jack.

"Jesus, what were you thinking?"

"Well… clearly, I wasn't," Jack said in a defeated tone of voice.

The server topped off Jack's coffee again and smiled at Caleb, "How 'bout you Sweetie?"

Caleb nodded and answered, "Same as this idiot."

She shook her head with a smile as she walked away to get his coffee and said, "You captains."

"Vitamin G," Caleb said. "Good choice."

"Yeah, well a Bloody Mary would have been better, but that's not an option today."

"Did you try to get someone to take your sail?"

Jack looked down at his plate, moved his fork around to mix the ingredients and answered, "No, I didn't want to sit in it all day."

"Probably a good call. Hey, I heard your Mayday yesterday – I was too far out to get there to help – was everything OK?"

Both men knew that mariners are required by law to render assistance, but it is a law that is wholly unnecessary. When a distress call goes out, everyone turns up their radios and tries to determine if they are close enough to respond. It's an unspoken pledge. When you are at sea, the only other people out there are others at sea. You are otherwise alone, and this isolation breeds the utmost loyalty among those given over to the waters. No one cares who you voted for, what you believe, or what color your skin is; if you need help, those who can help you, will help you.

Jack continued, "Just another drunk douchebag who couldn't follow instructions. He has a few stitches and a mild concussion as his souvenir from the trip," he said with a grin.

Caleb shook his head in disbelief, "It never ceases to amaze me."

As the two commiserated about the behavior of charter guests, Jack asked him about the fishing season, which Caleb said had been decent. The two continued the light conversation as Jack shoveled his way through the breakfast. By the time Caleb's mountain of food had landed, Jack had finished leveling his own. He stood up and started to pull out his wallet. Caleb caught the server's eye and waived his hand to indicate 'no', and then pointed to himself indicating that he would take the check.

"Put your wallet away, Jack, you've suffered enough for one day; I've got this one. It's the least I can do for hijacking your table and making you talk about dead fish when you're hungover."

The two captains grinned at one another, and Caleb knew that Jack was in no shape to mount a defense.

"OK kid, but the next one is mine," Jack said and then added, "Thank you – for everything."

Caleb had been somewhat of a quiet, grounding influence on Jack, despite the years to his junior. Jack's reinstatement as a captain running charters was a transition that he might not have survived, had it not been for these newfound friends in Point Loma. Even Caleb's unexpected appearance at breakfast had the effect of helping Jack reset after yesterday's events.

The two men nodded goodbye as Jack walked back out into the bright sun of another beautiful San Diego morning.

# VI

The captain emerged from the restaurant and squinted as he pulled his sunglasses down over his steel-blue eyes. After crossing Scott Street, he made his way down to the waterfront along America's Cup Harbor. Jack checked his watch and saw it was 9:20 a.m. The short walk to the docks of his charter company, *Sail this Bay*, would put him at the boat by 9:30.

"Right on time," he said to himself.

He smiled at his punctuality and mused about a captain's life being ruled by speed, time, and distance.

Now, the sunshine which he had cursed only a few hours earlier, felt like a gift as it glistened on the water and the brightly polished stainless steel adorning the superyachts. The waterfront was coming alive with sleepy tourists and eager sport fishing charter guests.

The tourists were the easiest to spot, often wearing brightly colored new clothes, some with a nautical theme. Their clothing bore no scars or memories of a life on the sea. Some of them looked like they were there for a photo shoot.

The fishing crowd wasn't too difficult to pick out either; they appeared like a pack of hungry wolves huddled around Styrofoam cups of coffee. Their apparel was somewhat less ostentatious than the tourists, but distinct. They wore old jeans and tee-shirts advertising their favorite fishing brand. Their hats proudly proclaimed the tribe to which they belonged, emblazoned with slogans like, *Look at My Pole*, and *Wanna Hook Up?* The heaps of gear and bags piled around them made it seem like they were going away on a long adventure. But, like most of the waterfront activities in San Diego, they were designed to detach you from reality for a short time at a reasonable expense, and then dump you right back into it later that day.

The locals usually wore faded tee-shirts and jeans, shorts, or bathing suits. For the men, a stained shirt was a badge that it had actually been used on a boat. Fiberglass resin, fish blood, bleach spots, and other unknown agents combined to create a tie-dye recognizable in boating communities worldwide. Women often wore sundresses that let their natural features spill out into the world around them. There was little pretense for those that called Point Loma home.

The tide came and went. The boats came and went. The people came and went. The predictable order created stability which Jack had come to crave. He sought to blend into all of it, to become part of the predictable order.

"Today is going to be a good one, Lefty!" he said to the pelican sitting on the piling he passed by. The large bird, known as "Lefty," had at some point lost his left foot and obtained the nickname. Lefty was becoming a celebrity as he appeared on social media and travel websites. About a year earlier, Lefty had claimed the piling in front of the tackle shop as his own. The fishing boat crews, and sport fishing tourists treated Lefty like a pet, and made sure he received plenty of fish scraps.

"You look like you are packing on a few pounds, old guy," he said to the bird who continued to eye him suspiciously.

As Jack approached the company docks, he unclipped the brass marine snap-hook from his waist and unlocked the gate. The tide was low, and he felt the incline as he walked down the steep ramp. He called out greetings to the other captains, Bradley, Ted, and Rob, as he turned his attention to the setting up of his forty-two-foot sloop rigged sailboat, *Zentimental*.

The routine which initially required notes and concentration, was now second nature to Jack. He quietly and quickly set about the tasks after throwing his briefcase on the sailboat. He began by flipping the breaker and unplugging the boat. He inspected the plug and receptacle, coiled the cord, and stowed it by the breaker. Then, he climbed aboard and unlocked the hatch. Once down below, he lifted up the cockpit cushions and bean bag chair, then he fastened the bean bag chair to the foredeck. Next, he unzipped the sail bag and prepared the lines before putting the winch handles in place. Finally, he checked the safety gear, completed the engine checks, turned on the radio, started the engine, and logged the engine specs. It was a morning religious ritual of great significance to him. The routine was predictable, and Jack had come to cherish anything predictable. This routine, Bradley's friendship, Lefty. Anything he felt would still be there the next day.

After the captain finished setting up the boat, he started hurling insults, "Did the barber slip, Teddy?"

Ted replied nonchalantly and without hesitation.

" What, you don't like my new look bro?" Ted said as he turned his face to the side and lifted his chin in a pose. Then, he hollered at Julie the dock manager, "Jules, I can't take my sail, Jack doesn't like my haircut – and you know that I can't live with that kind of rejection!"

Ted's laugh reverberated through the docks as Julie the dock manager glared at him. Everyone laughed and knew that Ted didn't care about what people thought of him.

"Children!" shouted Bradley.

"Thank you, Bradley," Julie said, "At least one of you is acting in an age-appropriate manner."

They were careful to stop the bawdy sailor talk before the guests started to arrive at the top of the gangplank – at least for the most part they were careful.

As the guests began to arrive, Jack and the other captains would start to size up the crowd. They usually fell into one of a few categories. Normal, nervous, nice, arrogant, and his most despised of all - poser. The posers wanted the captain and other charter guests to know that they had extensive sailing experience. They desperately needed to show everyone that they were in the club, despite having failed to pay dues or attend any of the meetings. Usually within minutes of boarding, the signs would emerge as the poser began interrupting the captain. Jack had given much consideration to this dilemma; by playing along, a tip was more likely, but sometimes it was intolerable.

Today's poser started the routine at boarding.

"Permission to come aboard Captain, and if you need any help, I've been sailing all of my life."

Jack smiled, "Thanks for offering to help out."

On and on it would go for the next three-hours. For the most part, Jack tolerated it with a sort of sadness. He reasoned, to pretend you are something you are not, and then to put it on display for others is truly sad, and sadness should never be mocked or celebrated. Despite Jack's sympathy, once in a while they would earn a rebuke; it was usually like a building storm.

His father often cited a centuries old maxim, *beware the fury of a patient man*. The captain would long suffer the fool on most days.

Not two minutes off the dock, the man asked, "Do you have a Six Pack or Master Near Coastal?"

Then, before Jack could answer he turned to the other guests and said, "The Master's test is much harder - most captains don't pass it."

Jack knew he was in for it, and while he gathered himself, he thought, I don't know how much of this I can take today, I may actually puke. The hangover now mixing with the poser's comments was unendurable.

"Actually mate, it's the same test - just ten additional questions. There are different requirements for sea service - the amount of time you've spent serving on a vessel, and where you were - inland, ocean, etc."

The crowd nodded as the poser re-positioned himself uncomfortably in his seat, then said, "That must be a relatively new change – 'cause I know guys that have taken both tests."

*Those guys were probably also full of shit*, Jack said to himself and decided to let the statement go unchallenged. Blend into the scenery, he admonished himself. Somehow, he tolerated the nonsense for the first two hours, until the man started calling into question the captain's choices about how the vessel should be rigged and sailed.

The wind had picked up to about eighteen knots and was gusting to twenty-five. They were headed back in and getting close to Point Loma. Like most land masses jutting out into the water, Point Loma worked its magic as the wind poured over the long finger of land, bending and accelerating the invisible force.

Jack knew what to expect, and how to prepare the vessel. He began to address the passengers.

"Hey everyone, I'm going to head up into the wind until I take some pressure off of the main, and then I will take in a reef – that's when we reduce the amount of sail area we are carrying."

Everyone nodded, and a few thumbs up were flown in a relaxed state facilitated by sun, alcohol, and sailing. Then someone asked, "Is it OK for me to get another beer?"

"Of course," said the Captain. "This is normal stuff, no big deal. I just wanted to let you know what we're doing."

Feeling reassured that there would be no disruption in their supply of refreshments, smiles returned to faces.

The captain expertly turned the sailboat toward the direction of the wind, but not directly into the wind, as he watched the leading edge of the main sail for the bubbles indicating the pressure was coming off the sail. When he had it, he set the autopilot and deftly stepped over and around the guests to the reefing lines and main halyard. Working one line in and the other line out, he brought the main sail down to its first reef point. After he re-secured the lines, he worked his way back to the helm and began to take in the genoa. The massive headsail began to roll around itself until it was about thirty percent smaller.

"That oughtta do," said the captain with a sense of satisfaction.

He had barely caught his breath and set course when the man started up again.

"We should have all of the genoa out - we'd be going a lot faster."

It was a bold statement, but people who have been lying for long enough can start to believe their own lies. People looked at the man, unsure if he was correct, then up at the captain for affirmation or rebuttal. At that point, Jack stopped caring about the tip. He knew that the time had come for him to wind the guy down.

"Really? Well, do you happen to know the calculation for maximum hull speed on a vessel?"

Jack had said it loud enough for the whole charter to hear him. There was an awkward pause.

"Oh, I'm not a numbers guy, never could remember that – what is it again?"

"Do you want it in imperial or metric?" Jack asked.

A stumbling non-committal answer came, "Ahh, imperial?"

Jack continued the exorcism.

"Hull speed equals 1.34 times the square root of the waterline length in feet." He paused for effect, and then asked, "Do you know the waterline of this vessel?"

"No," was all the man said.

Jack continued, "This is a forty-two-foot boat, with a waterline of thirty-seven feet and some change."

"Right, of course. That sounds about where I'd expect it to be," said the man struggling to maintain his dignity behind the walls and battlements of his falsehoods.

Jack pulled out his phone and performed the calculation, then continued.

"Take a look at the knot meter above, what is it reading?"

The poser looked around, unsure of what he was looking for. He saw a meter that looked like the right one, and taking a chance, he replied, "8.2 KTS STW."

"Yep, KTS, that's knots; we are going 8.2 knots STW - speed through water - which also happens to be the maximum hull speed of this vessel. More sail doesn't make you go faster in every circumstance."

He watched the reaction on the face of his guests as they contemplated this point of interest. Jack was starting to become hopeful that the lesson would result in a larger tip from the others to offset the one he was surely about to lose from the poser.

"We might exceed hull speed if we were surfing down the face of a large swell, or under the right conditions, surfing our own bow wave, but that's not here, that's not now."

Then he looked right at the poser, "It's Bill, right?"

The poser nodded in agreement.

"Don't feel bad, it's a common mistake made by amateurs who think that more sail always equates to a faster speed. Then of course, we also consider safety and comfort, right Bill?"

Bill looked down at the deck for a moment, put his head back up and somehow managed, "Thanks for the lesson, Captain."
"My pleasure, Bill."

Jack's work tearing down the man's ego was done, and he had taken no real pleasure in it.

"Come back here for a minute, would you mate?"

Bill got up and made his way through the labyrinth of legs and feet between him and the helm. Jack stepped out of his way and motioned for him to take the helm. He pointed toward the edge of Ballast Point.

"Keep us on this line. Be ready for some weather helm when it gusts."

Jack let the man settle in at his new post, while he tidied up some of the lines around him and chatted casually with a few of the other guests. Then, he walked back over to him and began to coach him gently.

"A little less correction, give the helm a chance to respond."

The man nodded, staying focused on his task. Jack could see his knuckles were turning white because he was gripping so tightly.

"Relax your grip a bit, she's not gonna run away on ya."

Then, the captain spoke gently, as if to a young child as he finished the most important part of this lesson.

"Bill, I'd like to suggest that exaggerating ability is never a great idea, but when you are on a boat, it's a terrible idea. Do yourself a favor, just be yourself and let people take you or leave you."

Jack looked deep in the man's eyes, which were welling up with tears, as Bill answered, "You're right, Captain. Thank you." Then Bill reached out and took the captain's hand in a firm shake.

After *Zentimental* was back at the dock, Bill was the last passenger off the boat.

"I had that coming, Captain. In fact, I've had it coming for a long time," Bill said as he stared into the wisdom he saw in Jack's eyes.

Jack looked at him compassionately and said, "I was too hard on you today – sorry, mate. You and your girlfriend come back out with me next week, it's on me - let me give you a real lesson."

Bill's face lit up from ear to ear and he said, "Yes, sir!"

Jack walked him up the gangway. Once they had reached the top, Bill turned around and reached in his pocket, palmed a handful of bills, and pressed them into Jack's hand.

"Thank you, Captain."

"Thank you, Bill! See you next week. Just tell the booking manager you are my guest when you make your reservation."

They turned away from each other as Bill walked away and Jack walked back to his vessel. Ted had seen the exchange.

"Everything OK, Jack?"

"Yeah, it's all good brotha," Jack answered.

Ted cocked his head and asked, "Good tip?"

It wasn't considered impolite to ask each other that question.

Jack shrugged, "I don't know, didn't count it."

Bradley called out loudly, "Beer anyone?"

Jack shouted back, "Count me in, Bradley. But no Mai Tais tonight; Jesus Christ, you almost killed me!"

Bradley laughed and smiled, "Was it really me or did you get into that good bottle of rum you've been hiding from me?"

Jack shook his head in disgust, "Shit, Bradley, you see through me like a jellyfish!"

All four of them laughed as Rob and Ted hollered back that they wouldn't join them that night.

"Pilot House?" Bradley asked.

"Beer and shrimp – yes!" Jack said as he smiled at his friend.

On this evening as on many others, Bradley would laugh, smile, and reassure Jack that all would soon be well. He needed to hear that over and over again, because it didn't yet seem real. He wondered on some days if he would ever feel normal again. He tried to remember what it felt like before the pressing weight on him began.

As he finished closing down the boat, Jack thought about Bradley. He didn't know much about his life before he became a captain. Bradley didn't offer any details and Jack didn't pry. Like himself, many on the docks had a story they did not want to tell. It was an unwritten rule, that you didn't ask unless you were invited. Jack invited no one to that conversation.

# VII

Later that week, the captain sat alone in a booth at *Portside Pub*. Normally he would have preferred a barstool and chatted with the locals, but recent events made him crave solace, although he knew that was the last thing he really needed. The pub sat along the main street running through Point Loma amidst other throwbacks to the sixties and seventies. There was an old post office, an independent drug store, a few marine supply stores, and some old liquor stores. Jack often wondered how the little town had managed to stay so innocent among the waves of gentrification that had washed over most of San Diego. It was only a few square blocks in either direction, and right next to the water, so it should have been an easy target for developers. *Maybe downtown San Diego kept them busy,* he thought to himself and considered the contrast between the redeveloped, modern downtown, and sleepy old Point Loma. Professional buildings housed older generations of doctors and dentists who still drove decades old European sedans, bought when they were young and needed to prove they had 'made it.' The doctors, like the town, now had nothing to prove, so they rested comfortably in the past. He sat and took it all in, endlessly mulling it over.

The appearance of Allie broke his deep train of thought. "Hey, Jack, you in there?"

She touched him gently on the shoulder. Somewhat startled, he looked up at her and smiled. "Sorry, Allie, I was thinking about something."

"Yeah? That was hard to tell, Jack," she said sarcastically. "Where the hell were you?"

All of a sudden, he was aware that he hadn't combed his hair after the sail and unconsciously ran his hand over his head.

"I dunno," he said.

"Sometimes, Jack, I think you are a force of nature, then other times you seem like such a sad sack of shit – I don't know which one is really you."

She smiled and they both laughed.

"I'm sure it's the latter," said Jack.

They laughed again. Her face turned serious, and she asked, "Have you eaten anything today?"

He shook his head side to side, and as he did so, her face turned into a disapproving smirk.

"Captain, I'm ordering you to eat something!"

This seemed to perk him up and he fired back in a mockingly formal tone, "By whose authority, young lady?"

"Mine," was all that she said.

This brought a smile to his face as she turned and walked over to tell the cook something. She knew him well enough that he usually just let her pick his food; they both liked that. Allie could feel that it was coming close to a date, but something always seemed to be holding him back. She contemplated it with frustration and remembered her mother's warning, "I'll never know why, but women seem to be drawn to rescue dogs and men with problems. Try to stick with the dogs if you need to rescue something."

As she walked away, Jack reminded himself that she was about twenty years his junior. It wasn't the number that bothered him. It was fear of the expectations that might come along with it, like late night dance clubs. He also worried about the gaps in cultural references and shared experiences over decades. Yet there was something about her that seemed to transcend her age and allay his concerns. As he watched her walk away, she started to transform into a woman from his past, then a mist, then she was gone. I can't lose her too, he thought to himself. Living and dying alone seemed to be a fair price to pay for the freedom from ever knowing that pain anew.

For Allie's part, she didn't care that there was an age difference. She liked it that he was older and settled. She reasoned that life experience could hold a guy on a straighter line. She looked at the captain and saw strength, stability, and tenderness. It was a combination that made him irresistible. He had tanned skin, salt and pepper hair, deep blue eyes, and a strong jawline that dared you to challenge him. She had thought about him more than once when she laid down in bed at night, allowing the fantasy to breathe and live within her. Yet, for all her boldness and independence, she wouldn't make the first move - not with him. There was an invisible barrier she couldn't understand because she knew nothing of him before Point Loma.

Jack knew that she was everything he wanted in a woman: fierce, brilliant, and the master of her own destiny. The captain wanted an equal, not crew, nor stew, nor first mate. He was old-fashioned only in the sense that he would hold a door, offer his coat, and let a woman go in front of him in a line. These were things that his father had taught him. His mother had taught him that a woman had to be tough to survive. He also realized that he had to say something soon or knock off the schoolboy flirting routine. While all of these qualities he prized were right in front of him, he struggled with the risk, and it haunted him whenever he thought about pursuing Allie.

Some people might have looked at Allie with her jet-black hair, piercings, tattoos, and thought, *Poor girl. Probably a single mom who made bad choices and now she's struggling to get by*. Their estimation was dead wrong. She had a bachelor's degree in philosophy from Stanford, paid for with a full ride academic scholarship. She lived on a boat she owned outright and worked as a waitress because it gave her the freedom to easily earn a few bucks before packing up and moving on. She lived to live. Her idea of living did not include a house with a mortgage, a car with a loan, and a 401K for "security." She needed to climb mountains, cross oceans, and forge raging rivers. She didn't own a TV, nor did she care about which Hollywood elite had been spotted at the latest club with someone else's husband. Seeing scandals on the news rack at a grocery checkout, she recalled the words of a philosophy professor, "Poor nourishment for the impoverished life."

After graduating from college with no debt, she took the considerable savings she had from working nearly full time while in school and started backpacking in the Pacific Northwest. A student of Thoreau, she was at home in the woods and content with only the belongings in her backpack. The end of the summer found her in Port Angeles, Washington. She fell in love with the old, storied port, rich in history. It was sleepy, charming, and somehow warm, in the cold and damp of the Puget Sound. The time-worn walls of clay brick buildings raised in the last century advertised, *The Only Cigarette that Starts Your Day*, along with miracle cures, and other "must have" items from long ago. The painted ads, like the town, mostly faded, could still be understood by the discerning eye.

Her morning ritual included a stop at Dock Master's Coffee, one of her only indulgences with her hard-earned money. On days when it wasn't raining, she would walk on the docks. The docks always reminded her of her grandfather. They had spent many days on his old wooden boat sailing on the San Francisco Bay. He had given her many gifts, not material gifts, but moral and practical ones. Hard work was learned sanding and staining teak, patience in waiting for a tide to change. Most importantly, he taught her the independence that founded her desire to set out on her own. He had circumnavigated the globe three times. She learned her independence from a man who had beat the system by never bowing to its expectations. He had died nearly penniless, the richest man she had ever known.

One sunny August morning as she walked the docks and sipped her cinnamon latte, she saw the boat that stole her heart, *Truant*. The forty-two-foot cutter was the first link in the chain that would ultimately lead her to Jack. The sailboat belonged to Captain Bradley.

Bradley had put the boat up for sale after cruising for several years. He was a man that believed in having at least two boats, but probably never more than three. He understood it was compulsion but reasoned that there were worse things to hold you prisoner. He had already beaten back some of those darker demons and restoring sailboats may have saved his life. When he had decided to move to Point Loma, he chose to leave *Truant* and sell her in Washington. There she rested impatiently awaiting her next caretaker.

There is often a deep and undeniable connection between the spirit of the boat and her caretaker. Bradley knew this connection intimately. His hands had lovingly caressed every inch of *Truant*. They had crossed oceans together, touched continents, and explored islands. He had turned to her on the last morning and said only, "Old lady, our adventures are over together, but many more lie ahead of you. Take care of yourself and your crew the way you took care of me." He turned away quickly and walked up the dock so that the tears he felt building would not be in her presence.

The sign read only, FOR SALE TO <u>LOVING</u> NEW OWNER, with his phone number listed below. Without hesitation, she had pulled out her phone and dialed the number.

# VIII

Jack noticed the rays of sun bouncing off the ocean outside of Point Loma and he languished in its warmth on this winter day. The sunny days never seemed to end – even through most of the winter. Southern California had been a good choice for him because it reminded him of the good times in Florida, but it was far enough away to ensure he never saw things that reminded him of her. It was also home, and home often has a way of making bad times seem better.

The wind had filled in, much to the delight of the charter guests and captains. Sails were full and spirits were high as the three charter boats headed out into the blue Pacific in search of grey whales.

Today, Bradley, Ted, and Jack would sail their small armada together. Captain Ted would lead, at the helm of *Sun Lover*, with Captain Bradley off his starboard stern in *Seaduced*, and Jack just off Bradley's starboard stern in *Zentimental*. Like three pelicans in flight, flying in half of a V formation, they flew gracefully, effortlessly, and with only a couple of dozen feet between each boat.

The captains applied years of skill in keeping the boats in this formation, controlling their relative speed to each other by trimming the helm and sails while chatting with the guests about anything and everything. The busy whale watching season was well underway and everyone could feel the energy and excitement. Today, Jack also carried with him a new captain who was seeking employment with *Sail this Bay* charter company. Jack had offered to take Captain Dave out with him for his final test, where the most important questions would be answered: Can he handle the boat? Can he manage the guests? Can he make interesting conversation? Can he add local color to the sail? They were quite particular about the skill set of their captains. After all those questions were answered, only one final, and most important question remained: "Would we like to sail with this captain?" Once, the dock master had said to him, "We don't hire assholes." Jack liked that policy and was glad they hadn't thought him one.

Captain Dave took the helm once they rounded the point, and the flotilla headed out toward the white and red vertically striped San Diego approach buoy bearing the letters SD, which marks the safe water entrance to the San Diego Bay channel. The wind was dusting the tops off of the small swells, producing a rich scene of white caps over the blue water. The usual comments began from the guests,

"Is it this beautiful every day?"

"Well, not every day, just most days," Jack said with a smile.

"Do you know how lucky you are that this is your office?"

"Ha! I never thought of it that way – but yeah, I'm darn lucky!"

On and on they went, mesmerized by the beauty of their surroundings, as the boats worked their way outside of Point Loma and into the Pacific Ocean.

Jack began to give them an idea of what they would look for in their search for whales.

"Sometimes you will see a large group of seabirds circling above the water and then diving in – this can indicate the presence of a whale or pod of dolphins - sometimes both. Look for spouts, tails, and if you're really lucky – breaches."

"There are a variety of whales that can be seen off the California coast, but the most common is the California grey."

He held up a small, plastic whale, and then handed it to a smiling boy who was wrapped in a lifejacket.

"These giants spend the summers feeding on the abundant fish in the Arctic, then they head south to mate in the warmer waters off of Baja California in Mexico. Folks, that's a ten-thousand-mile round trip journey they make every year! It's been fairly consistent this week, so let's all say a short prayer to Poseidon and ask for a good sighting. We should be close enough to see the barnacles!"

Then he leaned over to the boy holding the whale, and in a pirate voice he growled, "What think ye of that, young matey?"

The boy grinned ear-to-ear and resolved in his mind that someday he would be the captain of a sailboat.

Then, Jack worked in a little information that would be helpful for Dave on his own charters, "Most groups will at least see spouts, because you can see those from a long way off. The air in those massive lungs is hot, and when it mixes with the cold ocean air, it turns into a mist."

Dave nodded in understanding. Jack noticed that Dave was multitasking well. He was listening to Jack, glancing forward at the man up on the bow, and smiling at the cute ladies to his left. *He'll do just fine*, Jack thought to himself, then continued, "The luckier groups will get close enough to see the barnacles on the whales as they swim alongside the boat. It's kinda weird, but sometimes it feels like time itself slows down as you sail along next to them - like you somehow become part of their long journey," he paused in his discourse to make another sweep with his monocular. "I remember a breach," Jack began. "We were about a thousand miles off the Marquesas. It was a clear, calm day; the ocean looked like a giant lake. I looked forward off the starboard bow, and a massive whale breached - its whole body, tail and all. Then two more after the first. Of course, my phone was always down below. I dunno, maybe it's better to just see it with your eyes instead of the camera."

Dave nodded with understanding, and said, "Yeah, I've had that happen to me in the Sea of Cortez. It's that moment - hard to put into words, right?"

"Exactly," said Jack. "A moment to imprint a lasting memory for the mind's eye."

Then they heard the call, "Coast Guard sector San Diego, Coast Guard sector San Diego, Coast Guard sector San Diego, this is Fishing Vessel *Reel In*, over."

Jack and Dave were experienced mariners, they paused and turned their attention to the radio. Whenever someone was calling the Coast Guard, it was possible they needed assistance. After a brief delay, the radio crackled back to life.

" This is Coast Guard sector San Diego, go ahead *Reel In*."

"Coast Guard, this is *Reel In*, We just saw an adult California grey female go by that is dragging a large part of a fishing net – looks like her tail is stuck inside of it."

"Good copy, *Reel In* – please meet me on channel two-two-alpha."

Jack made a signal toward Captain Dave with his thumb and index finger turning an invisible dial in the air, indicating he wanted the channel changed to hear the conversation. Dave gave a nod in agreement and thumbed through the channels from sixteen to twenty-two. The guests grew silent and leaned toward the radio speaker, like a family listening to a radio drama before the invention of television. An impatient guest started to ask a question just as the radio conversation began, and the other guests shushed her before the captain even had a chance.

"*Reel In*, this is Coast Guard Sector San Diego, what are the coordinates and heading of the whale?"

"Stand by," came the reply from the captain of the fishing vessel."

Perhaps a minute passed; it felt much longer to Jack. Everyone remained hinged on what would come over the VHF radio waves next.

"Sector San Diego, this is *Reel In*, the whale's approximate coordinates are thirty-two degrees, forty minutes, zero-four-four seconds north, and one-hundred-seventeen degrees, sixteen minutes, zero-seven-two seconds west, traveling approximately one-hundred-seventy degrees magnetic, how copy?"

After reading the GPS coordinates back to the captain of the boat, the Coast Guard indicated that they would contact the agencies that would normally assist with marine mammal rescue. With that, both the fishing vessel and the Coast Guard signed off. Jack hesitated for a minute while he processed everything. He and Dave made eye contact and said nothing. It was clear both captains were contemplating the next move. A whale with an entanglement like that could die - they had both seen evidence of it - washed-up whale carcasses. Jack had recently read an article in BBC News claiming that an estimated 300,000 whales, dolphins, and porpoises die each year from injuries related to fishing nets and lines. Jack loved these creatures and felt compelled to act.

The whale was headed nearly due south. Without looking at a chart, Jack trained the glass on the area that should represent those coordinates, just off of Point Loma, outside of the kelp beds.

"Dave, do you see *Reel In* on AIS?"

After a brief pause, Dave answered, "Yeah, got em' - you should be looking right at them."

"I make that about two to three miles almost due north," said Jack. "What does the AIS read?"

Dave reached down and touched the display screen a few times on the chart plotter, "Right on the money, Jack. They are two point five nautical miles north of us."

Jack thought about the magnetic variances off Point Loma and did the math quickly in his head. Then he said, "Those greys swim at about five knots," and doing a quick distance, speed, time calculation in his head, he added, "I think she'll be at SD in about twenty minutes - she's probably not diving deep 'cause of the net. If that's the case, we have enough eyes and binoculars to keep her in sight." He paused again, and then continued, "I think we can be there in fifteen," he said, as he estimated their current speed and position in relation to the SD buoy."

Jack stopped and thought carefully about what he said next. He was directly, and legally, responsible for the guests, and yet he *felt* responsible to the whale. After so many years and tens of thousands of miles at sea, he felt as close to marine life as he did to most humans, sometimes closer. He thought about his recent track record and the injured guest, then he thought about the accident. Suddenly, he felt sick to his stomach as his thoughts came back to the whale.

"Fall off to a beam reach and head toward the safe water marker," the captain ordered.

Jack had made the decision with such an air of confidence that no one seemed the least surprised or concerned, and no one would question the command.

"Aye, Cap'n," was all that Dave said in response. Even though he also was a captain, he was not the captain of that boat on that day. This is a measure of respect shared among professional mariners - both men knew this, and no other words were exchanged about the matter.

"OK, crew - here's what I need you to do. Keep your glasses trained on that whale." - He pointed in the direction he wanted them to observe. Let Captain Dave know her position with your hand - like this." He motioned with his own hand in the direction of the whale. Then he disappeared below and reappeared in a few minutes wearing a wetsuit. He had a dive knife on his belt, along with a mask, snorkel, and fins in his right hand.

"Dave, she's all yours. Get me next to the whale, and if she appears like she will take the help, I'm going to get wet."

"Roger that," Dave answered.

Jack knew that it was common for marine life to seek out the aid of humans on the water. Divers, swimmers, and boaters all had stories about helping marine creatures. He had no idea whether or not this whale would want his help, but he felt like he had to try.

The captain continued, "Once I'm in the water, luff the sales a bit to slow the boat down. If she stops completely, just let the boat go into irons. If anything goes wrong, your priority is to bring these guests back safely - it is not to save me - comprendé, amigo?"

Dave nodded continuously while the captain gave the instructions. Then Jack turned to the guests, "OK folks, you are getting your money's worth today - I'm going to try to cut that net off of the whale. Dave will be your captain now until I return."

Jack had no illusions about the myriad of things that could go wrong. The average adult grey whale weighed sixty-thousand pounds. This was not a safe endeavor, but it was a risk that he had to take. He left the cockpit and took up station by the starboard shrouds as he searched with his monocular in the direction that the whale should be traveling. Just then, he heard the twelve-year-old boy shout.

"Spout - I saw a spout!"

Jack looked back and followed the boy's finger, then retrained the glass on that area.

"Got her!" He shouted. "Good work, lad! Duck down below and grab yourself a hat that says crew."

The boy jumped up. His mom tilted her head and widened her eyes, and without saying a word he realized he had forgotten his manners, and then said, "Thank you, Captain!"

Dave had already taken up a new course that in his estimation would help them intersect in about five minutes. Jack approved and gave him a thumbs up. They continued on that vector with the whale, and they were indeed closing.

Jack yelled back to the helm, "Dave, you OK with getting closer than we are supposed to?"

Dave shot a thumbs up back to him. Good captains follow rules, great captains know when they need to be bent or broken. In the final minutes, Dave maneuvered the sailboat more in parallel with the whale's course and started to match her speed by easing out the main and genoa. Jack was impressed with Dave's skills, and he looked back and nodded approvingly.

"Does this mean I get the job, Captain?" Dave hollered forward above the din of the wind.

"You're hired!" Jack shouted back as he stepped outside of the lifelines while holding on to the shrouds.

*Zentimental* closed to within ten feet of the whale. Everyone had moved over to the starboard side of the boat with phones in hand as they shot video and snapped pictures. One guest started to narrate:

"Our captain, a very brave man, is about to jump in the water to help this whale that has a net around her tail," she panned her camera from the captain to the whale and back.

Jack motioned to Dave with his hand extended outward and pressed down several times, indicating for him to slow down. Dave eased the sheets, and *Zentimental* slowed. The whale, now directly alongside, matched their speed. Jack made the motion again, and for the second time the whale also slowed down.

"OK girl, here's where ya gotta make sure I know what you want," Jack motioned back to Dave with a fist, meaning "stop."

Dave released the sheets, and the sailboat started to slide to a stop and drift in the direction the wind was blowing. The sails flapped loudly as Dave worked quickly to bring in the genoa.

Jack turned and yelled, "No engines, Dave - don't wanna startle her."

Dave nodded and continued his hand-over-hand work furling the head sail.

The whale was now at a complete stop alongside the sailboat and looking intently up at Jack with an eye the size of a baseball. He could feel it pleading with him. Without thought, he reached up and touched the ancient bone fishhook that never left his neck. It had been a gift from a tribal leader in the South Pacific, who had in broken English said, "You take this, for protect and luck, keep connected with the ocean."

Jack glanced back at Dave and nodded up, to indicate he was going in. He had slipped on the fins and mask as they had approached the whale. He pulled the mask down and fell backwards into the water next to a thirty-ton mammal. He felt the cold of the water on his exposed skin. Then he rolled over, and with only a few kicks of his fins, he was touching the whale.

"Don't make any sudden moves," he said as he patted the side of the great mammal.

She spouted and released some air. He hoped it was the equivalent to a sigh when you know that relief is in sight. He felt down below the water to the knife on his belt. Jack's dive knife was very sharp. It was far too small to harm the whale, but if he moved the wrong way, he could nick his own artery and bleed out before they could get him back on the boat. Keeping one hand on the whale to stabilize himself, and the other with a tight grip on the knife, he made a few flutter kicks to move him down the side of the whale toward the net. When his hand felt the net, he grabbed it and pulled himself up and out of the water a little by holding on to it. Then, carefully, with the blade outward and away from the whale, he started slicing the net. It was exhausting and his muscles strained to hold him in the best position. He kept talking to the whale, "A little more, girl, we're getting close. You're going to be a racing whale when this is done."

The huge creature floated motionless. It seemed to possess a clear understanding that he was trying to free her from the net that she dragged. It had been robbing her of energy and making it harder to feed each day. The whale, like the captain, was also exhausted.

As he got the net open, he brought his knees up against the side of the whale and used them for leverage as he worked outward and continued cutting. He could see that he was getting close to the last few sections when a loud horn with five short blasts could be heard coming from the channel.

"Shit," Jack said.

He couldn't see it, but he knew exactly what it meant. A big ship was heading out and heading their way - a ship who had right of way. His mind processed it quickly. He should have called a Sécurité - a navigational announcement to other mariners. Depending on what type of ship was bearing down on them, and its proximity, it might not be able to stop or turn fast enough. He looked back at Dave, who was already on the radio.

The ship was a San Antonio Class warship from the San Diego Naval base. Dave hailed the vessel.

"*Warship 17, Warship 17*, this is *Zentimental* off your starboard bow, over."

"*Zentimental*, this is *Warship 17*, we need you to move ahead a quarter of a mile so that we may pass by your stern."

"Negative *17*, I repeat negative. We have a man in the water, and he is providing assistance to a whale."

There was a long pause, and five more short blasts indicating danger. Few people said 'no' to the US Navy.

"Captain, please repeat your last."

Dave said more slowly this time, "We have a man in the water who is cutting a net off of a whale."

Warships can move quickly, and the boat suddenly appeared much closer.

"Roger, Captain, you are unable to maneuver, correct?"

He shot back, "Not in the technical sense, but yeah, we can't move - or at least not very quickly."

What felt like an eternity passed as some of the guests now began to panic and let out soft screams and cries.

"Oh, my god!"

"Are we going to get run over?"

Dave needed to reassure them, this wasn't great, but he could get out of it fast if it came to that. He wasn't sure whether he could get Jack back on board and get the boat out of the way - he needed that warship to alter course.

"Steady, crew - we can move if we have to - we've got the engine ready to fire up. I don't want to do it too soon because it might startle the whale and that could hurt the captain."

Dave could see that Jack was right next to the whale's massive tail; if that tale flipped hard, it could knock Jack unconscious, or worse. The moments between Captain Dave's last transmission and the response seemed much longer than it actually was. A stillness and silence overcame the group while they waited. Finally, the response arrived on the radio.

"Copy *Zentimental*, we are adjusting course and speed to pass your bow and reduce our wake. Let us know if you need any assistance."

The Coast Guard picked up on the transmission and began to broadcast a Sécurité navigational warning to other mariners. The captain on the bridge of the warship issued the orders and the crew expertly turned the boat away to the south and downwind of the sailboat, Jack, and the whale. Dave knew that they were lucky that it had been a warship and not a much less maneuverable car carrier. We were damn lucky in that - damn lucky, Dave thought to himself.

During the tIme Dave made the passing agreement with the warship, Jack had nearly finished. The guests were starting to turn their attention back to the whale, as they saw him cut through the last few cords of the net.

"He's got it, he's got it!" a college girl shouted loudly. She thought, *This guy is salt and pepper hot AND he rescues whales?* She whispered to her friend, "I'm getting the Captain to take me out tonight."

"That guy must have a girl, Tami."

"We'll see about that," she replied confidently.

Jack patted the whale a few times after he had carefully re-sheathed the knife. He then pulled the net underneath the huge giant until he could gather it up near him. Its weight was starting to get hard for him to manage and keep afloat, and he was trying to make sure he didn't get tangled and dragged down with it as the current pushed it toward him. He didn't want to let it go, in fear it would just snag another whale or dolphin. He was exhausted, cold, and now panting. Adrenaline helped him make a few more hard kicks away from the whale. He motioned to Dave with his hand like a key turning in the ignition. Dave understood his meaning and turned on the big diesel engine.

The whale, feeling its freedom once again, spouted, and dove gently, letting her tail come up in the air for everyone to see. Dave had seen Jack's difficulty with the net and had asked two of the guests to lend a hand with boat hooks - long aluminum poles used for docking or grabbing lines. Dave carefully brought the boat alongside Jack and put it in neutral as he signaled to Jack that he was ready.

Two guests stood ready with the hooks, a tall Texan, and a short young lady from Tennessee. They positioned themselves near the back of the boat. As soon as the net was within reach of the poles, they snagged it. "Got it!" shouted the Texan. Jack released it and kicked hard toward the swim platform and boarding ladder which Dave had lowered as they were waiting.

As the captain pulled himself back on board, he was shivering hard. The wetsuit he wore was a spring style, with shorts and no sleeves; it was hardly adequate for winter. A lady wrapped her fleece stadium blanket around him, and the college girl kissed him on the cheek.

"You're my hero!" Tami said.

*Subtle* he thought as he smiled at her.

"Well, folks, does anyone feel like they need to ask for a refund, or does this count as seeing a whale?"

They all laughed and spontaneously clapped and cheered.

He looked at Dave, "You mind watching her for a few more minutes while I warm up below?"

Dave bowed deeply and theatrically, "It would be my pleasure, Captain."

As Jack started to walk below, Tami said, "Do you need some body warmth? I can go down with you."

The middle-aged moms smirked disapprovingly, and the middle-aged dad concealed his approval. With her gorgeous blond locks bouncing in the wind, a never-ending smile, and twinkling eyes, he could barely say 'no,' but he managed.

"I'm not sure my girlfriend would approve," said Jack as he winked at her.

Jack figured a small lie would save her dignity.

It seemed to work until her friend said, "Told ya he wouldn't be single!"

Everyone laughed and Tami turned beet red.

Jack still wanted to ease her down.

"If I was single, I can tell you for sure that I would consider it my luckiest day if I was able to go on a date with someone as pretty and sweet as you."

At this statement, the middle-aged moms and Tami's friend let out a chorus of, "Aww."

He looked back at Dave and said one more thing before he disappeared below decks.

"This is one hell of a job, eh, Captain?"

# IX

Jack caught Allie's eye when they walked into *Portside Pub*, and she pointed toward the back deck. He smiled at her and nodded. He'd never really thought about how much he communicated non-verbally, but between Captain Dave, the whale, and now Allie, he was thinking he might be some kind of pro. As they walked through the bar, they stopped briefly to say hello to a few other sailboat captains - never fishing boat captains, except Caleb. That enmity was as old as the diesel engine, before which, sailing captains once ruled the fishing fleets.

The walls were covered with some of Point Loma's notable captains, and pictures of a few who had established their notoriety in a dubious fashion. The floor was old plank wood. It was never sanded or refinished, and it kept the memory of things that had hit it hard: beer bottles, belt buckles, pool cues, and a few knife blades. If it had been the seventies, the eighties, or even the nineties, the air would have been a thick cloud of smoke; its stains still showed yellow on the old, faded ceiling tiles.

Mostly men sat shoulder to shoulder on the bar stools, clad in sun-faded tee-shirts emblazoned with the names of their employers. Well-worn and tattered hats - some of which had circumnavigated the globe - were usually pushed up a little so they could still gawk at Janey the bartender while their face was buried in a beer. The smell in the air was a mixture of burgers, beer, and sunscreen. To Jack, it smelled like his youth.

The behavior of this group was anything but civil, yet it was all perfectly acceptable, and even expected. Between jabs at each other, the fishing boat captains bragged about their ability to find fish, and the sailboat captains bragged about the drunk passenger hitting on them that day, or the day before, or the day before that. The stories never changed much; it was a country club for women and men who work the sea. There was an acceptable dress code, language, and professional respect. The tourists and non-working boaters were easy to spot. Their clothes were newer, not tattered or sun-faded, and you could see them staring at the locals in admiration.

Jack held the door for Bradley as he smiled. It was odd that there was a door, because a ten-foot section of the wall had been cut out so that the inside and the outside were virtually one room.

"Age before beauty, Bradley, "Jack said as he smiled and stepped aside. 'It's obvious that you are suffering from hypothermia, Jack - confused thoughts - as I am both prettier and younger than you!"

Jack surrendered without a fight and started to walk in first, while taking a playful punch at Bradley's stomach.

"Yep - still hard as a rock!" Jack said as his knuckles dug lightly into the muscles in Bradley's abdomen.

They hadn't realized that Allie was standing behind them and had watched the two egos trying to walk through a door. She shoved Jack to the side and walked through first.

"This way, children."

They grinned sheepishly and obediently followed her instructions. There weren't many people these captains would 'snap to' for, but she was one of them.

"Another boring day on the water, boys? Here to drown your sorrows and bore me with stories about drunk passengers?"

Jack looked at Bradley and cocked his head, signaling with a slight nod that Bradley should take the lead on the telling of today's events.

Bradley began in an animated, theatrical style, "Allie, Allie, Allie, I'm so disappointed in you!"

"And why's that, Bradley?"

He paused and looked back at Jack before he turned to meet her gaze again.

"You think all that we do is ferry around drunk tourists?"

She smirked, "Of course not, Bradley, I know you host corporate team building seminars - real weighty stuff."

"Apparently," Bradley continued, "our friend Jack here is a marine mammal rescue specialist."

News normally traveled fast in the small port town, but she had just started her shift and had not heard about the whale rescue. Had it been twenty minutes later, no doubt she would have known about the rescue and rang the ship's bell for him when he walked in the pub.

Allie thought that Bradley was setting up a humorous ruse. "What? Is he moonlighting at Marine World so he can afford some decent clothes?" she said as she gently touched the well-worn collar on his polo shirt.

To Bradley and Jack's delight, they could see they had snared her. They looked at each other with impish smirks and cocked heads.

"Oh, Jack, she hasn't heard, why don't you tell her."

Jack paused and then said, "I went for a swim today on the charter."

"So what," she said in a sarcastic tone.

He cocked his head and smiled, "Rescued a grey from a fishing net."

"What? Oh my god! How, where?"

Bradley jumped back in.

"Easy, slow down girlfriend, let him tell you the story."

She carelessly tossed her tray on an empty table and slid into the booth next to Jack. She felt the well-worn vinyl stick to the back of her bare thighs and winced a little in disgust as she made a mental note to wipe them with hot water after the shift. Jack had her full attention as she waited impatiently for him to continue, "We were on our way out when…"

When he finished, she shook her head in disbelief, "Any other surprises for us, Captain? I swear, every time I think I have you figured out…" she trailed off and then said, "Wait here, boys."

She jumped out of the booth like a track star off the blocks and a few seconds later, they heard the ship's bell ring.

The ship's bell at *Portside Pub* was reserved for special occasions; new captains, retirements, births, marriages, deaths, and life-saving events. It hung on a section of old wooden mast that looked at home against the rough wood panels lining the walls of the pub. Everyone knew the bell was important and quieted down.

Allie proclaimed loudly, "Well, boys and girls, it appears we have a genuine hero in our midst. Captain Jack Kelly rescued a grey whale from a fishing net off SD today."

A round of cheers went up.

Jose, the owner, shouted, "Next round is on me, in celebration!"

The bar erupted in another round of shouts and applause. Jack and Bradley smiled at each other and sat while a handful of the captains, even the fishing boat guys, came back to shake his hand. They were all quick exchanges from the tough and macho crowd.

"Heard the call - nice work Skipper."

"You're a good man, Jack. I don't care what Bradley says about you."

They filtered through with congratulations until the beers on the house arrived, and then the pub returned to the business at hand – drinking and eating.

Bradley looked at Jack, "If you don't ask her out tonight I will!"

"You're gay, Bradley - how's that ever going to work?"

Bradley chuckled, "Well, you've got me there."

Jack sipped on his beer, wiped the foam from his lip with his open hand and shook his head, "We've been over this bro; I don't think I'm ready yet - I don't know if I'll ever be ready."

Bradley nodded understandingly,

"It's just a date Jack, not a proposal - you'll manage."

Jack nodded. He knew Bradley was right.

Bradley decided to lighten it up, "Whales mate, mate - maybe you should too."

He laughed at his own joke, as he hoisted his glass, "Here's to whales and captains getting laid!"

Jack smiled and tipped his mug to Bradley's as Allie walked back up.

"What did I miss boys?"

She did not like feeling out of the loop, or what her generation referred to as FOMO - fear of missing out.

"Jack's going to finally ask you out tonight, Allie, and you are going to say yes."

She playfully puffed up and said, "Am I, now?"

Bradley continued, "Do you have any other world traveling, whale rescuing, sea captains hitting you up on Tinder?"

She crossed her arms and scowled, "Hey, who says I'm on Tinder?"

Bradley put his hands in the air, "My mistake, my mistake, I thought you were BarFoxDom69. Mistaken identity - my bad."

She playfully smacked him on the back of the head. Without further hesitation, she looked directly in Jack's eyes, "Well?" she asked, as she waited for her invitation.

He tried to gain his composure, but he always felt like a high school freshman around her. Stumbling in an uncharacteristic way for such a confident man, he finally managed, "Allie, would you like to get a drink after work?"

"After three months of flirting, that's the best you've got?"

Jack's face began to slide from smug to scared. Even Bradley wasn't sure if she was joking. After a tense five seconds of glaring at him while he wished the net had taken him to the bottom of the Pacific shelf, she broke character and smiled.

"As long as you let me buy, hero." And then she simply turned and walked away.

Jack glared at Bradley, "You do know that I am going to kill you in your sleep tonight - right?"

Bradley sat back, spread his arms out wide across the back of the vinyl booth, "Totally worth it!"

The two men reached down and took a very long draw on the beers in front of them. Then, they picked up the menus like nothing out of the ordinary had happened that day.

# X

Jack Kelly had grown up poor in a wealthy area of Southern California. His family had not always been poor. His father had once been a successful entrepreneur featured in magazine articles, who laid thousands of dollars in cash on his dresser at night. By age five, Jack had traveled the world in first class luxury. But his father died just before his sixth birthday and left them no insurance or savings. The cash soon ran out, and his mother was forced to sell the home in which he had grown up. They sold most of their furniture and all of his mom's jewelry. They had very little left, once the debts were settled, and they moved into a cheap, run-down studio hotel room in San Clemente. In a sudden thrust of fate, he had lost his father, his home, and his friends.

The jarring reality of his childhood placed an indelible marker in his mind - one of poverty, loss, and uncertainty. Even today, the memory of a mostly empty refrigerator which usually held a quart of milk, a few slices of American cheese, half of a tomato, and flour tortillas, was a vivid reminder of what his childhood had been like.

Jack grew up working hard to gain a sense of control over his world. The jobs became a way to distract him from the thing that scared him the most - losing those he loved. He had never learned how to process loss, so it became a permanent fear wedged into his soul.

# XI

It was seven o'clock when Allie set the burgers down on the table and then said, "I get off at nine-fifteen, I intend to shower the stink of this place off me, and then you can meet me at the gate to G Dock in Sundown Marina - ten straight up and don't think you can be a second late." She handed him a torn hand ticket from her order book with her number.

"But Allie, what if the smell of this place is the only thing that makes me attracted to you?"

She leaned in, and in a husky, sexy, voice, offered him something to think about, "You like your girls greasy and smelly, Captain? I would have figured you more for the college cheerleader, tight shirt, short skirt, lace panties, and perfume," she smiled and leaned back out. "No problem, I'll leave the short skirt at home - and it's tougher to get to the panties through the jeans."

This one even made Bradley wince, "You're killing me, Allie!"

The three of them laughed as she walked away, and Jack said, "Jesus, Bradley, what have you gotten me into?"

Bradley picked up his beer, cocked his head to the right and grinned, "Heaven, Jack. I've gotten you into heaven."

Jack and Bradley's conversation trailed off as the food became their sole interest. As the ship's design on the center of Jack's plate became easier to see, Bradley was already mopping up the last drops of ketchup with his one remaining French fry.

"Be right back," Bradley said as he slid out of the booth and headed toward the bar.

Jack continued his work on the burger and fries, and soon could see the schooner painted on his plate. He noted that Bradley was talking to someone at the bar, so he slipped out of the booth and walked up to the front to pay the check, catching Jose's eye as he approached the register.

"All good tonight, Captain?" asked Jose.

"Always better than the last one - don't know how you do it, they are pure magic!"

"Thanks, Jack. I love to eat them, so I work hard to make each one perfect," he smiled with pride.

The captain handed him seventy dollars to cover his and Bradley's tab, "No change, the rest goes to Allie."

"I will see to it my friend."

"See you tomorrow," Jack said to Jose as he walked down toward Bradley.

Jack didn't want to interrupt Bradley's conversation, so he moved up behind him quietly and put his hand on the small of his back. Then he whispered, "The tab and tip are settled. Love ya man." Bradley turned and winked at him, and Jack went out the back door and began his walk to the boat.

Jack normally enjoyed the relaxed stroll back to his dock from downtown Point Loma. He would finish unwinding from his workday as he made his way along Cañon, past the small businesses that catered to the marine industry, in front of the towering condominiums which looked out of place at the edge of the tiny island, until the street rounded into Anchorage Lane, and then dead-ended into Shelter Island Drive.

Jack made good use of the time during the walk, lost deep in thought, his mind somewhere else. He often felt that each private moment was corrupted by memories he wished to neither have, nor lose. His thoughts mirrored his entire life since the accident: torn, confused, and tossed around. He had witnessed seas meet from different currents and winds; his soul had less direction than those confused seas.

The captain finished the last few minutes of the walk so deep in thought he almost walked past the gate to his own dock. Pulling the magnetic key card out of his briefcase, he tapped the gate and saw someone coming up the ramp. Jack held the door open wide and offered a pleasant, "Good evening," as another marina tenant walked by trailing a dock cart full of laundry, with a book, a box of soap, and a bottle of wine resting on top. The woman was in her early seventies, and her years on the water were easily revealed in the deep brown leather of her skin. She looked a little weather worn, but the beauty of her youth was still evident, and her body still firm despite the years.

"Plans tonight, Captain?" as she asked the question, she nodded down toward the laundry and the wine.

"Any other night, I would have been delighted to join you - but tonight I actually have a late date."

"My loss, her gain," she winked at him. "See you around Jack."

He smiled at her warmly, and then walked down the ramp to the dock.

Once Jack got to his boat, he began the careful preparation of himself and his wardrobe for the date. He laid out a pair of heavy weight khakis, a fresh polo shirt, and his best pair of topsiders. Then he prepared to shower and shave. He generally wasn't this self-conscious, but Allie made him aware of every smell, stray hair, and rumpled article of clothing. She was like a spotlight that chased away his confidence.

"Why do you give such a massive shit about what this girl thinks, Jack?" he asked himself as looked in the mirror and pulled his cheek tight, drawing the razor carefully over the soaped skin. He thought about the question again. *Maybe it's because she doesn't see me for the shell of the man I've become; somehow, she sees past my faults. And there's no denying that I'm crazy about her. I haven't felt like this in years.*

After he had finished his grooming and dressing, he glanced down at his watch. He had an hour to get to her dock; it was a thirty-minute walk, or a 10-minute car ride. He had time to kill, and empty time was not his friend.

# XII

Jack arrived a few minutes before 10:00 p.m. and watched her walk up the aluminum ramp to the dock gate. She looked amazing. The cool winter evening held a mist that created an otherworldly glow that lighted her appearance. Even partially obscured by the steel bars on the gate, she took his breath away. It was hard to believe that for the first time in over almost years, he was on a date. He felt very strange. The confidence that enshrouded him as a captain left him like an ebbing tide with each step she took. He could feel his breath shortening, and the flush on his face warming his skin.

As she came through the gate, he saw that she wore a light down jacket over a skin-tight black shirt, a faded and well-worn pair of jeans, and outdoor trail sandals with socks. If she had worn anything dressier, two things would have been true: she wouldn't be his type, and she wouldn't have been herself. Her jet-black hair bounced a little as she turned to close the gate.

"Hey," she offered him with a soft peck on the cheek.

"Hey back at ya, Allie," he returned the greeting with his trademark angled grin, where his right cheek lifted up more than his left cheek.

"You clean up well, Captain" she said as she looked him up and down.

"Thanks. I was thinking maybe *The Dirty Olive* - how's that sound to you?"

"Yeah, that sounds great. Do you mind if we walk along the waterfront first? I feel like I need the solitude after that busy shift."

"I'm always up for a waterfront stroll," Jack said.

They began walking along the concrete walkway that wrapped itself around most of America's Cup Harbor. The businesses and restaurants were long closed by that time of night, and it felt like they had the whole marina to themselves.

"Marinas are so peaceful at night," he began.

"I know, right? It's amazing."

"How was your shift?"

"Good night... except for these two asshole captains bothering me."

Jack almost walked into her ploy, and then realized as she smiled that she meant him and Bradley. He returned the smile.

It was an overcast December evening. The Santa Ana winds were forecast for the next few days, but they had not yet warmed San Diego. Allie was glad that she had grabbed her jacket - an often-forgotten article of clothing in the mild climate of Southern California. A pelican that had chosen a lone pier piling as its roost for the evening eyed them carefully as they walked past.

"Are you enjoying San Diego?" Jack asked her.

"Yeah, I like the weather a lot, and the people seem cool. You?"

"Definitely, although I feel like it's a stopping place, or a steppingstone if you prefer."

She seemed to ponder this before continuing, "Yeah, me too," she said. "Do you ever think you will find the place?"

Jack laughed softly, "I think I have found it and left it about three times already." He paused briefly before continuing, "I'm beginning to think that the right place for me is the journey to the place I think is right."

"Wow - very Zen," she laughed. "Yeah, I get it for sure. Maybe we're just wanderers."

"Maybe," he said.

They walked for a few minutes in silence, which for some might be awkward on a first date, but for them, it felt natural.

"Tell me about *Truant*," he said, "Bradley's old boat, right?"

"Yeah, and you know how meticulous he is. Everything is in Bristol condition and there is very little to do except ongoing upgrade and maintenance."

"Do you like the live-aboard lifestyle?" Jack asked her.

"Definitely. I'm 28, and I have no mortgage payment, I pay seven-hundred bucks a month for the slip, ten for electricity, fifty for boat insurance, forty for my diver to clean the hull, ninety for my cell phone, and one-hundred-ten for medical insurance. That totals a thousand bucks. After taxes, I clear about thirty-two hundred. I spend about four hundred on food and I eat for free at work. I have no debt, no car payment, and no other bills. That leaves me with about eighteen hundred a month I don't need to live on. I take three hundred for myself and bank the other fifteen hundred. Except for Christmas - I give it away. That's over sixteen thousand a year - I figure for every year I work and save, that's about a year's worth of cruising I can pay for."

"Smart," he said admiringly.

"How about you?" she asked.

"Kinda like you. I don't really spend much money - other than buying burgers to flirt with waitresses."

"Waitresses plural?" She asked in a mock accusatory tone.

"Ah, well… would you think less of me if I said it was only you?"

"Yeah, probably, it would seem kinda needy and desperate."

"Is this how it's going to be with you, Allie?" he smiled as he asked the question.

"Nope, I'm just warming up!"

They stopped the flirty exchange and he asked,

"How did you get the coveted live-aboard status?"

She smiled at his question and ran her hand up and down her nearly perfect body. "Do you really think there is a marina manager in all of San Diego that can say no to this? You'll learn soon enough."

Even though it was their first date, he had eaten so many Galley Burgers in front of her that it felt like the fiftieth date. He was comfortable in some ways, nervous and awkward in others.

"You can make fifty to sixty thousand running charters if you work hard for the tips, and six figures isn't out of reach if you do open ocean deliveries."

"Maybe I should become a captain," she quipped.

"Maybe you should. If you want to do that, I'll help you."

"How would you help me?" she asked honestly.

"Teach you the secret handshake," he said glancing down at her.

"I think I already know it," she said as she stopped and turned to him, holding up her middle finger.

"Yep, that's it - you're halfway to being a captain."

"Why don't you do the long deliveries?" she asked him.

"You're always showing up to a boat thousands of miles from where it's being delivered. The new owner doesn't yet know how badly he got screwed, and how many things that - according to the broker - just need a little elbow grease, don't work at all." He paused and let it sink in. "Then, you have to move the piece of crap across an ocean. Even when you're moving nice boats, it's never at the nicest time of the year. I did it for a while, but it felt like a real job - those captains really earn their pay."

"Unlike you?" she playfully prodded.

"Exactly," he said sarcastically.

They walked along quietly for a few more minutes. She had imagined that this is what Jack might be like, no bluster, no ego, no bullshit. She liked it that way. Allie was trying to be relaxed, but kept catching herself checking her hair, thinking about the last thing she said.

Jack interrupted her thoughts, "Time to cross the street - there's our bar."

*The Dirty Olive* was a holdover from the days of the Rat Pack crowd in the sixties. The building was a mid-century modern design, with all of the hopes and dreams of a debutante nation during a space age. It was now tired and faded, not unlike the hopes of the generation that was present when it opened. A huge, neon martini with a spear of three olives lit the building and the surrounding street. The foyer was separated from the rest of the bar, and it still had an old-fashioned coat and hat check. There was a continuous loop playing over the sound system, which was advertised for the last two decades as "recently upgraded." You were bound to hear Sinatra, Martin, Darin, or Davis belting out a song as you walked in.

Upon their entrance they heard Mack the Knife. Jack did a little slide shuffle as Bobby Darin hit a note and the brass drove it home. Allie smiled at his antics as they turned over their coats to the young man who also doubled as the valet.

As they walked in, they could see the wall of fame, with autographed pictures of celebrities and politicians. The chronology started to fade both in prominence and count by the seventies. After that, there were fewer recognizable faces and names. The unintelligible chatter of the small crowd filled the air with its murmur.

As they approached the bar, a tall thin man who had been watching them in the bar mirror turned around to face them.

"Hey, Allie Cat!" he said.

His friends laughed softly at the new moniker. The man who hurled the insult was Captain Mike Stanley, who ran a fishing boat well known for skirting rules and un-seamanlike etiquette of a captain.

"Fuck you, Mike," she snapped back.

"I see you got yourself a snail boat captain, hey Allie Cat?"

Jack ventured into it, "Well, Mikey," (he hated being called Mikey and all the captains knew it). "We can't all drive smelly stinkpots for a living. Is it true that you have been on a losing streak since September? I keep hearing that Mikey can't find a fish to save his life."

"Fuck off, Jack." He scowled.

Jack motioned her down the bar away from them and bent down next to her ear.

"Hey, if you want to go somewhere else…"

"Hell, no," she said defiantly, "That shrimp dick isn't going to ruin our date."

The bartender appeared and Jack motioned for Allie to order first.

"Grey Goose, easy vermouth, shaken freezing cold, four olives, nothing dirty about it."

Jack pursed his lips and cocked his head in approval.

"Same for me, Donny."

As the bartender walked away, she asked, "Should I be worried that you know a bartender at a martini bar by name?"

They laughed.

He was about to ask her a question when he saw Mike walking toward them. "Incoming," was all he said. She turned to face him as he started in.

"Allie, make sure you wear that tongue piercing when you suck him off."

He smiled evilly at Jack and said, "Jack, she's got a thing she does that…"

She cut him off, "Mike, you are such an immature asshole, I can't believe that I was with you for even a minute."

She had said it loud enough for most of the bar to hear. The patrons quieted down, and people turned to see what the commotion was about. Jack was ready to lay the guy out, but he also knew that Allie was fiercely independent; he feared the wrath he might incur if he tried to 'save' her.

Captain Mike thundered on, unfazed by the exchange.

"Well, Allie Cat, I'm sure that was the best minute of your life."

He smiled and turned back to his audience, who heard the shot and started laughing.

"It might have been Mikey, but you only lasted thirty seconds."

The bar burst out in laughter, and even his own crew decided to turn on him. One of them hollered "No Minute Mikey" and another, "Thirty-second thunder-less." He became irate and turned his anger back toward her.

"You bitch, I oughtta..."

Mike made the mistake of raising his hand to her. Jack slid between them so fast that Mike didn't know what happened as the web between Jack's right hand and palm shot into Mike's Adam's Apple. As Mike started to choke, the same hand had recoiled and formed into a knife-hand strike into the tall man's solar plexus. Down he went, gasping for air.

The normally quiet and kind captain bent over Mike, now on his knees, pressed his hand firmly on his shoulder and whispered in his ear, "Ever talk to her like that again, and I'll gut you with your own fillet knife - got it, Mikey?"

Jack pressed his thumb deep into the man's suprascapular nerve on top of his shoulder, causing him to wince and sink deeper toward the floor. Then, Jack's right hand slid down the man's arm, and took control of his hand by turning the wrist outward.

"On your feet, little guy."

The shooting pain in Mike's wrist seemed to magically lift him from his knees as he sought his freedom. Jack walked him back down the bar to Mike's crew.

"I think your friend has had enough; I know we have certainly had enough of him. Finish your drinks and get him back to his boat. I don't want to see him again tonight or it's not going to end well. We good here?"

The other captains sensed Jack's clear moral authority and nodded with agreements, "aye," "yes, Captain" and the like. They knew Mike had gone too far; too much liquid courage and its corresponding depletion of judgment had nearly cost him more than a blow to his ego. Jack had tempered his response so the damage was momentary. It was a choice he could have made differently.

Donny, the bartender, had set their drinks down like nothing had happened. He knew that Jack's long martial arts background left him with little need to worry. Donny had seen enough in his forty-years behind that bar that made this exchange seem routine and harmless. He smiled and winked at Allie as he walked away to fill another order.

When Jack returned to his barstool, they both started to blurt out a "Sorry" over each other, then fumbled for a few more minutes to regain their rhythm before deciding to move to an open booth.

"God, I am so embarrassed," she said when they sat down.

"Why? You're not the asshole, he is. He's the one that should be embarrassed."

"Yeah, but he said all that stuff and it's our first date, and now you probably think I'm some kind of slut."

He noticed her eyes water a little.

"Allie, I promise you, the only thing that I think is that he's an asshole. Let's toast to not being assholes."

After they clinked their glasses together and drank, he said, "Although, if I'm an honest man, I was kind of an asshole the other day to this charter guest…"

He told her the story of the poser he had 'taken to school' and the end result including the big tip. He confessed that he wished he could be more patient. She told him about a few off-color stories from college, and together they realized that they were not perfect and had no intention of pretending to be.

The relationship would start with honesty, but not complete honesty. Few relationships ever start with complete honesty. Jack wondered if incomplete honesty could really be called honesty. But he couldn't be honest with her yet, because he was still unable to be honest with himself.

# XIII

Allie was surprised when she realized that tonight would be their eighth date. She recalled the first one, at *The Dirty Olive*, and the unwanted appearance of Captain Mike. For some reason, this morning it really pissed her off.

"What an asshole," she said aloud to herself, as she recalled Mike's behavior while she jogged along the bayside walkway on Shelter Island as the sun emerged from behind the buildings in San Diego, and the morning air began to warm.

She knew that Jack wasn't telling her everything, and that was pissing her off, too.

"What's he hiding?" She asked a group of seagulls as she ran by them. They offered her no perspective. She was beginning to admit that her heart was in free fall for a man that she couldn't know, because he wouldn't let her in. As her frustration built around Jack's dodginess, so did her pace. She could feel her heart pounding harder as she sprinted toward the west end of the island and the Yokohama Friendship Bell. She dropped her pace to a trot for the last dozen yards, and then sat down on the steps leading up to the bell. This was normally the turnaround point for her run, but today she felt like she needed to sit down and take it all in. Jack had invited her over for drinks at his boat tonight before dinner. She desperately hoped that the time would be right to get it all on the table.

*Why do I feel like a high school girl on prom day? This is ridiculous. How did I let this guy get under my skin? I'm going to be thinking about this all day.*

As the sun went down that evening, Allie reappeared on Shelter Island, and met Jack at the top of the locked gate. Something seemed different to her, but she couldn't put her finger on it. As they climbed down the ladder on *Windborne* and into the galley, Jack casually said, "Grab a beer - top loading fridge left of the sink."

"You really know how to treat a girl right, don't you, Captain."

She was only joking, but it was enough to break through his zone of concentration.

"Sorry, Allie." He smiled at her sheepishly and sat down at the chart table.

Allie pulled out two beers and opened them on the wall-hung opener that was mounted above the counter.

"Here," she said as she handed him a beer as he stared at the chart, apparently drifting off to some other world.

"Did you bring me over here to show me how big your chart table was? Is someone compensating?"

Allie smiled and flashed her eyes to make sure Jack knew that it was a joke in good spirits; for some reason she felt like she was walking on eggshells, and that was not how she normally felt around him. It wasn't relaxed or casual anymore, it was focused and distracted - a strange dichotomy. It was a sudden change, and that scared her.

As she leaned over, she noticed that the top of the chart read NORTH PACIFIC OCEAN (EASTERN PART). Then further to the right, DEPTHS IN METERS. At the corner, and oriented along the right edge, INT 520. To the left of the title on the top she saw a ratio she had never seen before: 1:10,000,000. She pointed to it and asked, "That's a big number; what does it mean?"

"The 1 means one-inch," he replied before pausing for a few seconds, and then continued in a more Socratic fashion. "Any idea what the next number means?"

She thought about it for a second and said without confidence, "Ten-million inches?"

He nodded and smiled, "Yep, that's telling you the scale that the chart represents; one inch on the chart is the equivalent of ten-million inches in the real world. Any idea of how many inches are in a mile?"

They were both startled by a familiar voice behind them.

"Sixty-three-thousand, three-hundred-sixty - do I win a very cold beer?" Bradley answered and smiled as he climbed down the ladder.

*Windborne* had not been built with a staircase, a popular design among what Jack referred to as "Dock Yachts" meaning that they were best suited for entertaining friends at dock.

"Hey, Bradley!" Allie said excitedly as he came down the ladder.

"You know where they are, help yourself... matter of fact, I've been meaning to ask you, did some of my beer end up in your belly a few days ago?"

"Guilty as charged - the liquor store on the corner had a flood and closed early - I viewed that as an extreme emergency."

"God, I can't imagine what it must have been like for your parents when you were in high school."

They all laughed.

"Oh, it was pretty bad," Bradley offered up. "In fact, one time, we actually raided my grand-pop's whiskey."

"You dirty snake, Bradley!" Allie shouted playfully.

"It was the caper of a lifetime my friends. First, he only drank one shot a night before bed - kept it on his nightstand - so we couldn't raid the bottle in his room. But he always kept one in the pantry as a backup - good Irishman that he was. The seal was intact on that one, and that was the safe we had to crack."

"How'd ya do it?" Jack asked.

"We heated up the tea kettle, and when it started to steam, we held the bottle over the steam so the seal would peel away."

"Son of a bitch, you are a crafty one, Bradley!" Jack snapped back.

"We poured out half the bottle into a mason jar and then watered his bottle back to full."

"What about the seal?" Allie asked him.

"Ah yes, the touché finale," he said with a French accent. "We super-glued the seal back on - it was a cork plug, so no broken metal ring."

A group of seagulls began chattering that sounded like laughter to the punchline of his story.

"Did you hate your grandfather?" Jack asked shaking his head from side to side.

"No, he was an amazing man, and we loved him dearly. He was an Irish Immigrant who supported his family of five working hard in a nursery his entire life. His whiskey was one of the only pleasures he ever indulged in," Bradley said solemnly.

"So, you took away his one pleasure? Bradley, even for you that is extreme debauchery!" Jack snapped.

"What happened after he opened the watered-down bottle?" Allie asked.

"Yeah - what about that?" Jack echoed.

"We were in the family room when it happened, me and my cousin Johnny - he was the one that helped me steal the booze. All of a sudden, grand-pop's voice thunders from his bedroom, in his thick Irish brogue, 'Goddamnit, Mickey' - who was my aunt - 'What the hell happened to me goddamn whiskey!'"

The three of them laughed.

"So, my Aunt Mickey takes off to the bedroom. Me and Johnny figured we were toast. We didn't say a word; we stared wide-eyed at each other and sat there in silence until she came back. I mustered up the courage to ask her, 'what's wrong with pop's whiskey?' - we all called him 'pop' - she says, 'no idea, he says it doesn't taste right. I opened it for him myself and it was sealed tight. We'll take it back to the state store and return it on Monday.'"

"You never got caught?" Jack asked.

"Nope," Bradley said with finality.

"You know you're going to hell," Allie said as she smiled at him.

"At least I'll know most of the people when I get there."

They all laughed again, then quieted down as Jack reoriented himself over the chart.

"What are you looking at Jack?" Allie asked.

Jack pointed over to the bottom left side of the chart.

"Hawaii - wanna go?"

"Who me?" she asked in a shocked tone.

"You," he pointed at her, "and you," then pointed at Bradley, "and one more victim yet to be named - maybe Teddy."

"I can do a one-way with you, but not the whole loop down and back," Bradley said.

"Who said anything about coming back?" Jack said with a devilish smile, and then turned his attention to Allie, "What about you?"

She felt a lump in her throat, and her skin flushed slightly.

Jack sensed her discomfort and offered, "Something to think about - no need to decide now."

Allie nodded in understanding. She appreciated him taking her off the spot and knew that he had not intended to make her uncomfortable. It was all somewhat confusing to her, though. They had just started dating and here he was talking about leaving; but he also invited her to leave with him. Was it the sailors equivalent of "will you move in with me?" She also had no way of knowing if he had been planning this for months, or if he was running away. It bothered her greatly that she did not know these things. She really liked to know things.

As Bradley and Jack chatted about charts, Allie sat quietly lost in thought. She thirsted for adventure, but had planned on crossing oceans alone; was this a bridge to that future of complete freedom, or was it a prison? Then she thought, *I'd be nuts to pass up a trip with an experienced captain and instructor, right?* Then she wondered, *maybe that's where I have to go to learn about him.* All of this rushed through her mind while Jack and Bradley talked about prevailing winds and squalls. She poked around the saloon looking at his books: Hemingway, Steinbeck, Slocum, Thoreau, Melville, Dickens. "Interesting," she murmured to herself. She was trying to blend into the background to give herself time to acclimate to all of this new information; then she saw the box. She picked it up, opened it, and took out the picture on top - one of many pictures of the same person. The face that stared back at her was so beautiful and peaceful. Who was she? Neither Jack nor Bradley had mentioned a woman - but he was in his mid-forties, so it made sense. Allie grew curious. Her need to know was about to kick into overdrive. Almost without control over herself, she turned and held up a picture towards Jack and asked, "Who is she?"

Jack and Bradley turned toward the unexpected question looking directly at her, then they looked at each other. Bradley found his escape hatch quickly.

"OK kids, time for me to bolt— I think I hear my mother calling." Bradley did not like conflict or confrontation.

Jack shook his head in disappointment that Bradley had decided to leave. Bradley had seen and handled thirty-foot seas - he was no coward - but he knew that this was a course they would need to chart on their own.

As he scurried up the ladder, she was starting to regret the question and knew she had let her curiosity get the better of her.

"I'm sorry, Jack - really sorry. It's none of my business and I shouldn't have been poking around in your stuff."

"It's OK, Allie. She was someone I cared about a great deal. It's been a few years, but it still hurts. Can we just leave it at that for now?"

"Of course. Again, I'm so sorry."

She could see the pain on his face, and though she wasn't very maternal by nature, she felt so much empathy for him. Something about his face seemed so distorted. It was like she was looking at a different man. In the instant that she asked the question, she saw the ocean crossing captain and all his confidence disappear. What remained was a hollow, tired, and tortured soul.

She walked over and put her arms around him and said only, "Forgive me, Jack."

# XIV

It was already March. Winter had flown by with a busier than usual whale watching season. As the season slowed down, he started taking fewer shifts on charters, and began chipping away at the project list on *Windborne*. Still planning to take the long sail, a lot needed to be done. On a boat, something always had to be done.

Jack remembered what an old sailor had told him, "The work on the boat is finished after you have gone bow to stern and worked every project. Then, you get a break," the old man had chuckled. "A break between the time you walk from the stern back to the bow and start over. On my eighty-foot Ketch, I can stretch that walk to nearly a minute!" Jack could still hear the man's husky, tobacco strained voice, bursting into laughter.

There were many logical reasons that non-boat owners would give Jack about why owning a boat was a bad idea: depreciating asset, cheaper to rent than own, or just throwing your money away. There was only one reason that Jack would give in response, "When I'm on the boat, the rest of the world slows down and fades away." For him, that made all of it worthwhile – all of it except the loss and pain he had known. Yet, he felt *Windborne* was still his home. More importantly, it had been her home. He had nowhere else that felt like home – for Captain Jack Kelly, there was no choice but to stay on *Windborne*.

He loved to watch the non-boaters on a three-hour charter. They would make the jokes about the expense of boat ownership on the way out. Then, on the way back they would ask about the price of boats and moorings. As the sun melted away, the jokes they had made earlier turned into understanding. "Now I get it – why you do this." He had heard that more than once. The transformation was sudden and powerful. The profound change often wore off as quickly as it had arrived, as the fences of their day-to-day lives re-erected themselves. Some people allowed those fences of confinement to remain indefinitely. They had been convinced that they needed a minimum of two-million dollars, rental properties, social security, and a mortgage-free home before cutting ties with their paycheck – what they saw as their "security." Every financial planner alive would agree with their plan and think Jack's insane. The captain knew this and paid it the attention he felt it deserved. He knew that true security lived in his relationships and not his bank account. He presently felt very wealthy.

Over the last few years, Jack often thought of his work as a delivery captain. He had seen the futility of living an entire life for a future that was not guaranteed. One delivery he would never forget was particularly heartbreaking. A man at seventy had finally achieved all of his lifelong financial goals and ordered a well-appointed yacht from the factory. Before the boat was delivered, he was diagnosed with terminal cancer. He never even took delivery; a yacht broker re-sold it to fulfill someone else's dream. They had the means to buy the boat twenty years earlier but had thought it to be imprudent. Jack knew as well as any thinking person does, that life was a transient friend who should be conversed with each day. Putting off that conversation is merely the denial of our mortality.

Allie, Jack, and Chris, a new friend from the marina, sat huddled around his saloon table looking at a small, portable, dry erase board that Jack used for teaching. Underneath it lay the sailing chart he had shown to Allie.

The captain looked at the group and began the discussion.

"The Pacific High is a large high pressure system that sits off the west coast of the United States – well it doesn't actually sit, it moves."

He paused for a moment while they absorbed the information and then he laid out other details about the passage, and how they would have to come north around the top of the Pacific High to about the latitude of San Francisco, to get back to San Diego.

Allie hadn't needed too much time to decide after he asked her about making the passage; when they got together for coffee a few days later, she had said, "I'm in." Bradley also had agreed to make the trip over, so the captain had his crew to Hawaii: Allie, Bradley, and Chris.

Jack felt good about the dynamics of the group. In his estimation, experience was nice, but cooperation was better. A mentor had once told him to pick crew carefully because, "Once you're out there, if it sucks, you're stuck." The next chance to get them off the boat might be two, three, or even four weeks away.

"I'd like to look for a weather window as early as mid-June, so we will need to have our shore responsibilities wrapped up by then," Jack said with finality. "Now the most difficult question of the day... Where should we eat lunch?"

As they contemplated their meal, Jack began to put away the charts. As he opened the cabinet, Allie saw the box again. They hadn't spoke of it again since the first time that she had asked. It was hard for her to not know the answers. It was very hard for her to not ask the question again. She wondered if he would talk about it once they were out on the ocean. She felt uneasy and began to wonder if any of this was a good idea at all.

# XV

By early June, the project list was considerably shorter, and it was down to a few items that still needed attention before *Windborne* was ready for a passage. The boat had been hauled out, cleaned, and inspected, and then given a new coat of bottom paint. After she was back in the water, Jack personally inspected every inch of standing rigging that held the mast upright. While making the inspection, he recalled the night when it was nothing but a tangled mess. The chaos. Suddenly, he almost screamed her name. His heart started to race with his mind in the past and he forced himself back into the present.

The doctor had said it was post-traumatic stress disorder, or PTSD. He had heard of the term for returning war veterans, but he hadn't known other types of traumas could cause it. Jack had the telltale signs: memories forcefully invading his mind, avoiding the eastern seaboard of the United States, deep guilt about the event, and an extreme self-loathing that had never been present before it happened. He might have never known about it, except he overheard another captain, who was an Iraq war vet, talking about veteran suicide and his own journey to recovery from PTSD. His friend got him in touch with a doctor, and Jack initially tried some counseling, but gave up because he didn't believe that he deserved to be healed, so he remained anchored in a sea of guilt.

# XVI

When Jack next saw her, she was leaning against the steel railing above the seawall, looking down at the elegant heron foraging for food. The tide was low, and the long-legged bird walked effortlessly through the exposed bay mud. The marine layer was spilling down over Point Loma into La Playa Cove like a mist coming off of dry ice. Allie was wearing the same tattered pair of jeans she had worn on their first date, tucked into an old pair of sheepskin boots, and a faded green sweatshirt bearing her alma mater.

"Her ass in those jeans…" Jack murmured to himself as he walked toward her from the parking lot and then called out to her, "Hanging around the docks again trying to pick up a real sailor?"

She spun around with a smile on her face, "Sure am, you know where I could find one?"

"Ouch!"

"Hey, you started it, Captain."

"Yeah, I did," he said with a smile.

As he closed the last few feet between them, she turned around fully and pressed herself back into the bars, leaned back and said coyly, "I guess you'll do."

He slid his strong leg between hers so that it pressed up into her firmly, while his arms enfolded her. As their lips met, he could feel so much more than passion. He was both happy and terrified to have these feelings again.

"I wasn't expecting to see you tonight - what happened to work?"

"One of the girls needed to switch a shift, so I'm off tonight."

"A free night and you chose to spend it with me?"

"Yep, that's right - you're one lucky guy."

"Believe me, I know."

They kissed again, not as long this time, but just as hard.

"I bought some new sheets for the aft master: wanna feel how soft they are?"

"Subtle," she chuckled. "How long have you been saving that line?"

They laughed as he took her hand and led her to the gate. Even though she had the gate key he had given her, she also respected his independence. More than that, she still sensed that invisible line. She could see it, feel it, and even hear it in his voice. It was always the same message, *Don't get too close to me.*

They made their way down into *Windborne's* saloon. The boat's interior managed to strike a nice balance between traditional and modern. There was plenty of real wood with lighter coloring, so it felt bright and cheerful. The saloon was well ventilated with four hatches that also allowed in plenty of natural light, which was now fading as the sun ducked below the peninsula.

"Drink?" Jack asked her.

"Sure, what'd ya have in mind?"

"I've perfected an evolution of a whisky sour."

"Oooh, sounds yummy, what's the evolution?"

"Key lime instead of lemon - I call it *Captain's Key Lime Cooler.*"

"Is it served with a handsome captain?"

Jack answered the question with a grin and the raising of his eyebrows. He began pulling ingredients out of the cabinets and laying them on the saloon table in front of him: Irish Whiskey, Key West Lime Juice, simple syrup, and two eggs.

After he had all of the ingredients laid out before him, he walked across the saloon and reached into the cabinet that held the ship's glasses. He paused for a moment as he realized that the last time he had used them was with Jen, over three years ago. He took out two glasses and a shaker and walked back to the galley.

He placed everything on the counter and started measuring the ingredients in a shot glass before pouring them into the shaker. Then, he carefully broke each egg over the shaker, holding in the yolk as he let the whites drip into the container. Finally, he filled the container with ice and then began shaking it vigorously. When he finished, he poured it through the strainer into the heavy crystal glasses etched with the boat's name. The egg white created a froth that held the taste and aroma of the smooth drink.

Picking up the glasses, he joined Allie in the club style chairs on the starboard side of the saloon. He handed her a glass as he sat down.

"Cheers," said Jack.

She took a long pull from the glass. After she had swallowed and savored the moment, she remarked with amazement, "Wow, that is dangerously smooth."

"It's a spin on an Irish buddy's whiskey sour recipe, except when he pours you one, there are four full shots - his should be named *Trouble on the Rocks*."

"Or maybe he should call it, *Shipwrecked!*" she said enthusiastically.

Allie looked down at the heavy crystal glass, "I've never seen these come out before; why tonight?"

"I dunno, we..."

He stopped himself just in time.

"I only use them on special occasions."

But she had caught the "we." Allie took another sip and then said, "Jack, you know that you've got to tell me eventually - right?"

"I know. Not tonight though, OK?"

"Fair enough."

They sat quietly for a few moments, sipping their drinks.

"So, if you only use them on special occasions, what's so special about tonight?"

"I guess it feels like a special occasion anytime I'm with you Allie."

"Wow, that's a beautiful thing to say Jack Kelly; I had no idea you were..." she trailed off of her thought. Then she set her drink down, got up and walked over to him.

She bent over and kissed him again, it was a long, deep, kiss. Then, she ran her hand across his crotch; she could feel him coming to life very quickly. He slid his hands inside her shirt along the bare skin of her back, and she trembled with excitement. After a few minutes of her tender lips on him, she stood up, took his hand, and led him back to the aft master.

"Time to feel those sheets," she said.

Jack seemed to be all at once, inside of her, under her, on top of her. He kissed her body from her mouth to her feet. She felt his warm mouth pushing against her. She wanted all of him.

112

But she could still feel that distant part of him, holding something back - even as they explored each other so intimately.

When they had finished, he held her in his arms, and they drifted off to sleep as the sound of an unbound halyard pinged rhythmically against the side of a mast somewhere on a neighboring sailboat. The last few gulls hanging around for a meal made a fuss about something. As she drifted off, she could hear him snoring lightly.

Allie woke up to the sound of a soft thud around five in the morning. She could hear that the wind was building, and the boat had bumped up against its fender as a gust came through from the south. Jack had slept right through the noise. She was warm and it felt so good to be next to him. Allie knew that she had fallen hard for him. Her bladder was the final force of nature that brought her out of the warm berth. She slipped out quietly into the head and sat down on the toilet, "Brrrr," she uttered as her bottom hit the cold plastic.

A foggy summer night in San Diego could still be chilly as the moist air found its way back to the ocean. When she had finished, she retrieved her jeans, sweatshirt, and sheepskin lined boots and walked into the saloon to put them on.

Allie normally enjoyed the peacefulness of mornings in the marina; but on this morning, she felt uneasy and corrupt. Her intention was to go through the box that she had seen a few months ago. Curiosity had gotten the best of her as she walked across the invisible line drawn by Jack.

With a glass of sparkling water in front of her, she opened the box and started going through the pictures. There were pictures of him and the woman in Key West and Bimini. It looked like most of them had been taken with an old thirty-five-millimeter camera, because the box also held small plastic containers with rolls of film.

Allie thought the woman in the pictures was stunningly beautiful - far prettier than herself. The shots showed white sand beaches, gatherings with friends, what appeared to Allie as charter guests posing with the captain, and many pictures of her when it seemed she did not know the shutter was flashing. Jack was admiring her beauty and trying to capture it on film, and he had managed the near impossible.

Jack had slept in, and when he finally awoke, he found her still sitting at the table with the box of pictures. His face said to her without speaking a word - 'Why?" She couldn't apologize this time as she had months ago. They were so much closer now, but Jack was still hiding something from her. This awareness brought tearful questions, "Who was she, Jack? What happened to her?"

# XVII

"We started in Fort Lauderdale," Jack began.

Allie let that sink in for a second before responding.

"How did you end up in Fort Lauderdale, I thought you had always been a West Coast guy?"

"I had just gone through a bad breakup and decided I needed a new start. I'd been to Florida a few times, and I had some friends doing day work in the yacht industry - washing, waxing, that sort of thing. I called one of them up and asked if I could crash on his couch while I got myself established down there. I sold all of my belongings, and my car, packed a duffle bag, and hopped on a train headed east."

"Why'd you sell your car?"

"It wouldn't have made the trip across country," he chuckled.

"Why a train?"

"I don't know, there's something about the click clack of the tracks and the passage of time that seems to heal me. Flying would have been cheaper and faster, but more expensive in the long run."

"How do you mean?"

"More expensive to my life - I was devastated. Staring out the window of a plane for six hours was not going to be any sort of remedy. Staring out the window of the train for five days helped me arrive in a more settled state of mind."

"Ahhh," she answered. "What happened with, you didn't say her name?"

"Dana. She began to change; suddenly she wanted a very different life than I envisioned. It started after she went to a self-help seminar on 'success.'" he framed the word with air quotes.

"One of those get-rich-quick buying and selling property deals. Next it was the bottle blond hair. She had the most gorgeous, natural, chestnut color hair... It would get sun bleached each summer. Then her tan darkened, and her freckles came out." He paused again for a moment, then continued, "After she became enamored with the culture surrounding that group of people, she tried to hide the freckles with makeup. As if her natural beauty wasn't good enough anymore."

Allie interjected, "You don't strike me as the kind of person that would dump me if I bleached my hair."

"I wouldn't. All of that was just the tip of the iceberg. She started amassing a mountain of debt, leveraged every nickel possible. Her life became consumed with flipping houses, making new and super phony rich friends, and going to their boring cocktail parties."

"Yuck," she said, having never been one given to pretension.

"That's what finally blew it all up. I was at a party listening to these assholes tell me about the private schools their kids attended, and how unfair it was for them to pay taxes that went to public schools. Of course, you'd be listening to this bullshit on a five-million-dollar yacht, or a rooftop deck above a fifteen-million-dollar home on Lido Isle. Like the tax they paid after all the loopholes was anything more than a rounding error on their income. So, this particularly obnoxious guy starts telling me how he took advantage of a widow whose husband had left her with nothing - no insurance, no pension, nothing. He recounts a story of how he screwed her over, 'We can list your house for sale' he told her, 'but the market has slowed down a bit. It could sit for months. If you lose it to the bank, you'll get nothing.' After he finishes the story, this evil smile blossoms on his face, and then he says, 'the dumb bitch took twenty-five percent less than market to do a cash sale the same day. I sold it within forty-five days and made a hundred grand.'"

Allie's eyes grew wide in disbelief that people actually could behave like this toward fellow human beings.

"I looked deeply into his eyes, and Allie, I swear to God, you could see the man had no soul. Then I said, 'You feel good about taking money from a widow?' He was stunned that I had said that to him. He just stared at me with his mouth hanging open. I set my drink down, looked him in the eyes again and said, 'I don't belong here.' I walked outside, called a car, and went home."

"Did you tell Dana you were leaving?"

"No, and that may be the best part - that guy told her - he was apparently offended. When she got home, she let me have it with both barrels, and made it clear that I would not embarrass her like that again."

"What happened after that?" she asked.

"I didn't say much in response. I figured, what's the point? She's chosen her path, and it was time for me to choose mine. I packed a duffle bag and walked out."

"That must have been awful, Jack."

"It was. But it needed to happen. It would have all burnt down eventually. The sad part was that she had been so pure - down to earth - before she bought into all that shit. I guess one day she woke up and decided that eating out at our favorite burrito food truck and sitting on the beach wasn't enough anymore. That I wasn't enough anymore. I think that hurt more than losing her - my worth had been determined by the balance of my bank account."

"Are you still in touch with her?"

He winced at the question.

"She's dead. When the real estate market crashed in 2007, she was too heavily leveraged, and she lost everything. She killed herself."

"Oh, my god, that's so sad."

"The worst part about it is that those pricks who run the seminars just reinvented themselves. Then it became about finding foreclosures. A new way to plunder during a period when people's lives were falling apart - capitalism at its finest."

"They all can't be bad; aren't there some entrepreneurs in there, too? Just hard workers?"

"Sure, they're a part of the mix. It just doesn't sit with me when people profit from someone's loss - it doesn't feel right. I guess that's my problem."

"It's just who you are, it's not a problem - at least not for me."

She smiled and winked because she could see this trip down memory lane was not one that he wanted to take, and they hadn't even gotten to the photos yet.

"So, these pictures aren't Dana are they - 'cause I see you two on boats, and in Key West."

"Yeah, that's not Dana, that's Jen."

His countenance darkened and he sat quietly for a few moments.

"We met on a superyacht. We had an immediate connection, but I've never been someone who can just ask a girl out. It takes me time."

"As you've clearly demonstrated with me," she said with a smile in an effort to help lighten his load.

"It was even more pathetic than that, Allie. I used to hang around the docks near her yacht hoping to bump into her."

He laughed softly as he recalled his adolescent behavior, "I felt so awkward around her, but also so comfortable; how does that happen?"

"I don't know, Jack."

Then he told her how Jen had ended up in Fort Lauderdale, after rejecting the path laid out by her parents.

"She said to me that at some point she started to feel dead inside. Like she was just going through the motions. Life had become boring drudgery even though she appeared successful to others."

"What did she do before she was a stew?"

"She was a lawyer, believe it or not. That came in real handy when we set up our business. When she had finished paying off her school loans and car, she sold her condo and stuck the money in the bank. She quit the firm that was working her to death and moved from Orlando to Fort Lauderdale and began to work on yachts as a stew. Her parents lost it. You could see that her whole life had been laid out for her - at least in their mind. What a sick thing it is to impose your own will on your kids."

Allie nodded in agreement and stayed silent hoping he would continue.

"She was amazing - so much discipline. She worked her ass off and saved every nickel she could. I guess I never thought about it, but in that way, you two are very much alike. Eventually, we managed to both get hired onto the same yacht. I was a deckhand, and she was a stew. We worked on the boat for two years. I worked my way up to mate, then I took my captain's test. We saved every dollar we earned with the goal of buying this boat." He looked around *Windborne*.

She saw him start to tear up. She slid in next to him and put her arm around him, "Let it out."

"Part of what had held me back for so long was that I was always tormented from losing my dad so young, being afraid to lose my mom, losing everything we had. It left me running hard in no particular direction. I was just sure I had to keep running."

Jack had suddenly switched topics from Jen to his childhood, which surprised Allie, but she felt a sense of relief that she was finally getting to know the man that she already loved.

He trailed off and the room was quiet for a minute, except for the sounds of the sea birds. Then, he started again.

"Why does everyone expect you to be a certain way? Why can't you just be yourself? I think that's one of the reasons that Jen and I connected, we were both trying hard to be ourselves. Why is that so hard for some people?" Jack looked into Allie's eyes as he wiped his own.

"I don't expect you to be anyone else, Jack, I swear to god I don't."

"I know," he said.

"Bradley and Ted don't expect you to be anyone but yourself either. I think it only feels like it's everyone when it's people that have such authority or influence over us."

"Wise beyond your years, Allie. Jen had felt that pressure from her parents - or maybe, some of it was self-imposed - I guess we can't blame everything on our parents. She had a foster brother that crashed and burned. He ended up in a lockdown mental facility. It really screwed them all up. She struggled with a ton of co-dependency… she felt like it was all on her shoulders to be a success, to make it all seem worthwhile for her parents. We went to their house one Thanksgiving. I remember how she tried to justify all of it to her parents. The tension in the air was heavy. They gave her the usual lines about financial security, and then added that she should get this foolish playtime over with and get back to the real world."

"Deep programming," was all that she said.

"Huh?" Jack responded.

Allie went on, "It's the message of society that is drilled into us at every turn: go to school, get a job, buy a house, start a family, vacation in Hawaii. We hear it so much that we don't even realize we've been programmed. It may be someone else's reality, but it doesn't have to be mine," she said with firm resolve.

Jack continued his narrative, "Her parents had once been unconventional. Hell, that's what led them to adopt the boy and that choice had nearly torn their family apart. I think I'm drawn to unconventional - I suppose it's why I love Teddy so much."

A knock on the side of the boat caused both of them to look up the companionway.

"Hey, I just heard my name - I told you not to talk about me on Tuesdays or Thursdays!"

And then came the thunderous laugh. It didn't matter to Ted whether or not the joke was actually funny to anyone else. It was so powerful that only those who were dead inside wouldn't join him in laughter. Jack and Allie joined in.

"Come on in Captain, oh my Captain!" Jack shouted over his trailing laughter.

As Ted's tanned face appeared in the opening, his smile burst through the tense moment and jolted them from the somber mood. He answered back with gusto quoting Walt Whitman's poem, "O Captain! my Captain! our fearful trip is done, The ship has weather'd every rack, the prize we sought is won."

They smiled at him as he reached in the cooler for a seltzer water.

"Of course, you would know that, Ted," Jack said.

Ted cocked his head, paused for effect, and said, "What, doesn't everyone recite nineteenth century poetry?"

Amused at his own wit, he burst into laughter which forced them away from Jack's painful past.

"Jack, I saw the guy in the khakis and striped shirt again today," Ted declared with a measure of disdain. "I think he has a closet full of them. What kind of douchebag dresses like that?"

Jack shot back quickly as he motioned up and down to Ted's outfit, "What kind of douchebag dresses like this?"

"Your mom likes the way I dress, Jack— we've been over this."

"You're a sick puppy, Ted," Allie said playfully.

"He's not dating my mom, Allie," Jack said in a parental tone.

Ted came back quickly, "If I marry her, Jack - and I may - you will absolutely call me daddy. And when I say, who's your daddy? you'll say, 'You my daddy, daddy.'"

Ted's laugh reverberated off the walls of the sailboat saloon. This time Allie and Jack just shook their heads with smiles, realizing that with Ted it was best to buckle up and enjoy the ride.

"Ok, I can only take so many mental images of you with my mom, dude - let's get back to your ridiculous outfit. You look like one of those swamp alligator wranglers in Florida!"

Allie laughed and Ted playfully glared at her. The outfit in question was a pair of cut-off blue jeans, a sleeveless tee-shirt with small lobsters, and a beat-up straw cowboy hat.

"You don't like my threads, bro?"

"They seem out of place for a charter captain in San Diego, but whatever shines your dime, buddy."

Allie excused herself and went into the head.

"How was your sail yesterday?" Jack asked

"Bridal Shower - three phone numbers."

Ted was the youngest of the captains at the charter company. He stood about five-foot-nine and was very fit. He had a rugged, handsome appearance that matched his profession. His good looks, deep tan, and sense of humor made it easy for him to meet women on the charters. He started wandering around the boat, examining everything with his innate curiosity. He somehow divided his time between a full-time job as a charter captain, a crisis counselor, and a volunteer helping the disabled sail, yet he never seemed to be in a hurry. If you were broken, he didn't mind. If you thought too highly of yourself, he would patiently tolerate you. If you felt alone, he would assure you that you were not, unless it was by your own choice. His spirit seemed to emanate from the universe itself, and yet he remained happily unaware of the powerful effect he had on others.

Ted would never be mastered by another, and his ethos seemed to come from within. Jack thought to himself as he gazed at his friend, *I guess that's what draws us to him, the unmistakable conclusion that he runs his own life*. Jack saw the freedom that surrounded Ted, and being himself imprisoned in his own mind, he envied it deeply.

The two of them chatted for a few minutes about the docks: who had done well or been screwed in tips, the latest antics of the owners, and the work that needed to be done to the charter fleet.

As Allie walked back in the room, Ted interrupted himself and winked at her playfully, "So, what are you and the pirate wench doing after the sail tonight?"

Ted and Jack were doing a special corporate sunset cruise that afternoon.

"Well, Allie likes to parade me around places with millennials so she can show them how lucky she is to have found a real man - you know, one with a job. You should come out with us; you'd fit right in since you live with your mom and play video games all day."

Allie and Jack laughed while Ted put up a mock protest.

"Hey! I don't live with my mom and play video games all day, OK? OK?" He paused for effect, then continued, "I play them at my friend's house who lets me sleep on his couch because I can't afford my own place!"

This time the laughter seemed to disturb the sea gulls lurking nearby who burst out into squawks and squeals.

"Do you really sleep on your friend's couch?" Allie innocently asked.

"Allie!" Jack pleaded, "He'll never stop if he thinks you believe him. He doesn't sleep on his friend's couch; he sleeps in his car - he doesn't have any friends."

The three of them laughed.

"Yeah, that's true, Allie," he said. "Ever since you hooked up with Jack, I've been on my own. I miss snuggling with Jack."

His devilish smile left her wondering whether or not he was joking.

"Jesus, Ted, is there a line you won't cross?" Jack asked him half-seriously.

"Nope!" said Ted with enthusiasm.

"Seriously, you should tag along - see if one of those bridesmaids wants to go. They're probably all drunk and sobby 'cause their friend's getting married and they don't even have a boyfriend."

"Aarright - I'm in!" he said, then added, "but I be wearing this!" again theatrically posing to show off his outfit. He burst into laughter one last time and disappeared as quickly as he had appeared, hollering over his shoulder in the voice of a teenage girl, "Text meee!"

Allie stood up.

"I should go too, Jack. I've got a breakfast shift at the pub. Will you eat before the sail?"

"Yeah, I'll come into the pub, there's a waitress there that's got me wrapped around her finger."

"That's SERVER Jack!"

She slapped his face playfully.

"Stop talking like a Boomer."

"I'm not a Boomer!"

"Is that what you really wanted to say, Jack?"

She playfully glared at him.

"Sorry, I meant to say, yes ma'am, won't happen again."

"Ma'am? How old do you think I am?"

"Oh god, what have I got myself into? Ted got you all wound up and then he just left."

She leaned over and kissed him softly on the mouth.

"Thank you for starting to share your story," said Allie.

"There's a lot more and it gets a lot worse," Jack said in a defeated tone of voice.

"I know. It's OK Jack. I'll see you later."

She grabbed her backpack off the nav station and climbed up the ladder to the cockpit, where she disappeared from his view.

Jack sat alone in silence for a few minutes and thought. *I'm glad that Ted showed up when he did, I don't know if I could have gone any further today.*

Jack thought about the darkness. He recalled how tangible it had been, like a thick fog that clouded his vision. He realized that Allie and Ted were in the light – the light he desperately needed.

# XVIII

As the sun began to set on the horizon, the captain placed the boat just outside the point, where he hove-to. He had seen thousands of sunsets over the ocean and reminded himself that no two were the same. Every one of them was a moment to experience. He thought to himself, *When I am old, this is what I will remember as my life ebbs away.*

The boat got quiet. He changed the music from a pumped-up party mix to a soft and soulful song. Cameras came out, ooohs and ahhs began, and *Zentimental* rested in the gentle breeze. Even Jack's turbulent mind became still.

His phone buzzed. Ted had texted him some pictures of the sunset. He smiled and thought, "so millennial" of him. The phone buzzed again. *So amazing, bro*, was all that it said.

Ted had a vibrant passion for life. He lived it with such intensity that it lit a spark in those around him. It was as if a furnace inside him only needed a small push of air from the bellows before exploding into a raging fire. The neighbor of "Hey bro" was "Go fuck yourself." He transitioned between them effortlessly. Unruled, unconstrained, unlimited. In Jack's estimation, Ted was like the sea itself. It reminded Jack of his own youth. Although, he thought himself to be wiser now, but also weary.

Another text from Ted snapped him back to the moment and out of his deep contemplation, *Dude, look behind you! It's him!!! WTF???*

He turned around and saw the guy in the blue striped sailor shirt, a traditional black Greek fisherman's hat, and khaki pants. He chuckled inside as he returned the text.

*Cool, let's ask him if he wants to go out with us tonight… Jack* hit send.

The response was instant, *Don't you dare Jack!*

*Standby, hailing him on 16 now…*

Jack sat with a smug smile on his face while he waited for his friend to realize that he was the victim of a prank.

*I will NOT go to a bar with that guy Jack!*

*Sure you will, we'll all wear striped shirts.*

The radio stayed silent. Ted heard no hail for the oddly dressed captain, and he realized that his friend had effortlessly wound him up. A string of anger emojis from Ted came next, and Jack continued smiling at the thought of his friend. He swung the boat onto a port tack and made a line on the inside of the green channel markers, well outside of the channel, and aimed for the piling outside of the Coast Guard station at Ballast Point. It was his favorite part of the sail, and he would pit his skill against the changing conditions, always with the goal of a one tack sail. He'd tacked when they turned to come back in, and that was the only tack he intended to make today.

The warm winds from the desert made for a very comfortable, forty-five-minute sail back to the harbor. As they approached the entrance to America's Cup Harbor, he spun the boat into the wind.

"Alright friends, now's the time I start the fabled Dance of the Water Buffalo again, as I hop over and around you while I bring down the sails. Keep in mind, *Sail this Bay* will not accept any financial liability for damaged paint on toenails." The guests laughed.

"And, If the boat moves and I have to grab onto something, it might be you - my hands tend to follow my eyes. So, if I've been looking at something I might just grab it!"

They laughed again as he paused for effect, "I am, of course, talking about your elbows - I have a real thing for elbows."

More laughter came from the very relaxed, and mildly intoxicated group.

The boat sat nose into the wind as he locked the wheel in place. He liked to bring the sails down at night without the motor on - let the boat drift quietly as he plied his trade. The captain deftly stepped over and around the guests as he brought the mainsail down into its stack-pack and worked the zipper forward from the back of the boom to the mast. He did this while constantly looking around for approaching boats, sea kayaks, the occasional suicidal paddle-boarder, and while answering questions from his guests.

"…Yes, there is a great sushi place just off the docks."

"…The taco place is Rita's; I'll point it out to you on the way in."

"…Which boat? Oh, I'd say that one is about seven million or so."

"…Sure, I can replay "Sailing" one last time as we are docking."

"…A slip here ranges from five to fifteen hundred plus a month, depending on the size of your boat, and which harbor it's in."

He told them a short story and started to wind them down; their sail was over, even though they wanted it to go on forever.

*Sail this Bay's* docks were sandwiched tightly between several multi-million-dollar yachts. As they came in and out of the docks, they generally only had a few feet of clearance on either side of the boat. Backing in at night was always interesting, and though he had done it hundreds of times, he made his approach as cautiously as the first time. He would have to be careful tonight because the wind would blow him off the dock toward Ted's boat.

He slowed the boat down outside of the narrow opening, looked behind him to see where Ted was, and seeing that it was all clear, he turned the boat one-hundred-eighty degrees as he prepared to back into the slip. With her stern facing the opening, he put the boat in reverse and began increasing the throttle. He waited calmly for the motion of the boat to restore his control of the helm while the wind and current continued working on the boat's angle and drift. He expertly anticipated the boat's next movements with a slight adjustment to the helm.

During this three-minute process, the captain's concentration was at its fullest on not hitting the yachts crammed into the small commercial dock. His guests were unaware of how delicate the maneuver was and continued firing off their questions, as if the captain had nothing else on his mind.

"Captain, what did you say to eat at Tahiti Tom's?"

"Coconut Shrimp and one Mai Tai only!" Jack answered.

The boat began its approach toward the slip.

"Is there a good steak place?" another guest asked.

"Yep, right across the street; I'll walk you to the top of the dock when we're done."

The captain stood facing backwards and quickly glanced to his right to assess the distance from the yacht. Two feet, he thought to himself. The wind blew almost directly from the stern of the boat at its current angle. He held the boat pointing almost directly to the dock, knowing that as soon as he started the turn, the wind would begin pushing the boat away from the dock. The questions continued.

"Is that the beer place you told us about?" asked a young lady.

"Yeah, that's it," replied Jack.

"They have bathrooms?" she asked with some urgency.

"Yes," he said.

Now he thought to himself as he answered the question and began the turn.

"Do they serve food?" someone else asked.

"Charcuterie, that kind of thing," he answered

Twenty feet to the dock, he noted while continuing to answer the barrage of questions and processing all the moving components that affected him: boat speed, wind, current, rudder angle, and prop walk.

"What's your favorite beer?"

Slow the boat and ready the line was in his mind as he said, "Get the hazy IPA."

"Ooohh, I love those," said one of the men.

*Neutral*, he thought as he shifted the boat, turned the wheel harder to starboard, and brought the port side of *Zentimental* alongside the dock. He glanced back and saw the immediate effect of the wind on the bow, pushing it away from the dock. The boat drifted backward and began to come off the dock. Then, at just the right moment, he expertly tossed the line down and over a dock cleat, and then with a whipping motion, caused it to cross back over itself. He made the line secure on the rear cleat, and quickly moved back to the throttle control. By now, his bow was only inches from Ted's boat. It wasn't in any danger, but there was certainly ego involved and it would cost him a beer if he hit it - that was the rule. *Forward*, he thought as he throttled the boat forward, causing tension on the aft dock line. As that line became tight, it caused the boat to spring back toward the dock. As the boat finally stopped, it was perfectly lined up with the boarding steps on the dock. The charter group clapped and exclaimed,

"Wow, I can't even park my car like that!"

"Can you teach me to do that?"

"I've docked a lot of boats in my life – so smooth."

"Yeah, and he did it while answering our questions!"

The captain humbly responded, "Thanks for the kind words, everyone, it's just a part of the gig."

Then he helped the group gather their belongings and disembark. He walked the blissful guests up the ramp and off the docks. A few of the girls hugged him. One gave him a kiss on the cheek. Promises were made to see him next year. Finally, an envelope with a tip was discreetly handed to him from the group leader with a firm handshake and warm smile.

"You did exactly what we needed you to do, Captain Jack. Helped us decompress and get closer as a team. Thank you, sir."

"My pleasure, Jeff, anytime."

The gate closed and the clean-up began. It wasn't the most glorious part of being a captain he often thought to himself, but in his final estimation, they were dues well paid to be a part of the club.

# XIX

It was pure coincidence. The man in the bathroom stall happened to be seated in silence when he heard the voice of the man in the stall next to him. He could only hear one side of the phone conversation, but it was enough to tell him everything he needed to know.

"Yeah, tonight. *Tequila Storm* - downtown… Yeah, that's the place… No dude, call a ride home - you don't leave there sober, well, I will, but you won't!" The laugh tore through the tiled bathroom with a loud echo. "Me, Allie from the Pub…yeah, the hot one, and Jack… Captain Jack Kelly… you met him at my thing… Yeah, cool, 9:00 is good. Gotta bounce before I flush… Yeah, from the can, man - classy right?" A softer laugh this time joined by the sound of rushing water.

The man sat quietly as the unknown stall-mate finished and washed up. He sat there for some time and thought about the past. It was a daily struggle for him to keep the past in the past. It had a way of creeping into his mind. But the name Jack Kelly brought it back like a tidal wave.

He never thought he would see the man again after the day of the hearing. He certainly had not looked for him. There were times he had fantasized about killing him. His rational mind would stop him because he realized that wouldn't bring her back. What he didn't know, nor could he know, was if it would make him feel better, or if some type of divine justice would be served. He thought to himself, *she's dead, and you're down here sailing in the sun?*

There was a darkness that he had experienced after her death. In that long night, he did think a lot about killing Captain Jack Kelly. He felt like he had little to lose after losing so much. Gradually, the staff at *Key Breezes* inpatient treatment facility helped him find his way back from that valley.

Now, his mind began to race. The thoughts came closer and closer together with less and less context. After drifting for so long, meaning and purpose came into focus. It felt good. He felt energy, like before the long, dark, period. Before the medications. *Did I forget to take my medication today? Yesterday? I think I have forgotten them all this week. But I feel much better. Yes, that's why everything seems so clear now. I'm better, I don't need them anymore. That's the decision, I won't take them anymore. This is better. I feel alive - like I could climb a mountain. Jack has got to pay for his crimes. We all have to pay for our crimes. That's the word. The word of God. I can hear his voice again - like before the darkness.*

Then a rhyme came to him.

*Captain Jack, don't look Back,*
*For it's me you'll see, on that we can agree.*
*There's a price to pay, your bill is due today,*
*No payment plan, I'll collect in full my man.*

Yes, this was so much better. He could feel it - all of it. He could see everything. The past, the boat, the storm - all right in front of him on the wall of the bathroom. He could hear her

136

scream. It was so loud in his head that he put his hands on his ears and started screaming himself. He screamed at the top of his lungs. The sounds echoed harshly off of the tiled walls and steel doors.

Yet, he knew he hadn't been on the boat that night. In his mind it was real, and he was struggling to keep reality and fantasy separate. They blended together effortlessly like oil on a canvas, creating new and interesting colors in his mind.

A few seconds later, a server stuck his head in the bathroom and said, "Hey, everything all right in here?" The man calmly opened the door of his stall and stepped out, "Yeah, sorry, just saw how much I lost in the market today."

"Hey, can I ask you a question?" The man said to the server.
"Sure."
"Do you know *Tequila Storm* downtown?"
"Yeah, why?"
"I'm meeting some friends there tonight and I want to surprise them - is there a back door by any chance?"
"Yeah, there's a place to smoke just off the alley. You can slip in through that door."

The server nodded a goodbye and turned to leave the restroom. The man took his time, washed up, and walked into the bar. Then he heard the voice that had been in the stall next to him and followed it to a barstool.

He looked carefully at Ted. He made mental notes of his physical characteristics as he walked by him, slow enough to take it all in, fast enough as to not look suspicious.

His mind began racing again. *If this was Jack's friend, then he is a friend of the devil. Maybe he should pay a price, too?*

*Here they are going out for a night on the town, while she doesn't even have a proper grave!*

Faster and faster the thoughts now tore through his mind. *How many, oh lord? How many must die to avenge my angel? I'm so sorry, lord, I've been absent from prayer - it was those damned pills! I won't take them anymore.*

He hadn't been a particularly religious man before her death. Loss has a way of driving us to find meaning in the events of a universe filled with random chaos. Yet, there is order. How chaos and order fit so cleverly together was a question he could not untangle. He had tried for so long. He had prayed for endless days and nights before finally hearing God's voice.

*I never should have taken those pills in the first place.*

Inspired and feeling ordained by God, he spun around and walked back toward Ted.

"Excuse me, are you one of the captains that works with Jack Kelly?"

"Yeah, man."

"Great! Is he still running charters for... oh, hell, what's the name of that company?"

"*Sail this Bay,*" said Ted.

"Yes! That's it! Do you happen to know if he's taking a boat out tomorrow?"

"Yeah, bro. We're all out tomorrow. Might still be a seat or two available, but I'd check first thing in the morning."

"Most perfect! Hey, he's an old friend from Key West and I'd love to surprise him - sunglasses and ball cap - like a disguise. Then, somewhere underway, I'll do the big reveal."

"Hell yeah! That's awesome, bro"

"Here's a couple twenties - buy Jack a drink tonight and tell him you ran into an old friend of his."

"How'd you know I was going to see him?" Ted asked suspiciously.

"Sorry, didn't intentionally eavesdrop; I was in the stall next to you while you were on the phone. Heard you say Captain Jack Kelly," he leaned in and cocked his head with a smile, "figured that no just god would allow two of them on the earth!"

"Ahahahahaha," Ted's thunderous laugh rang out again. "Sounds fun - I'm in! Anything to have a little fun with Captain Jack!"

Ted took the two twenty-dollar bills and folded them in half before slipping them into the pocket on his shirt.

"See you on the docks tomorrow, Ted, have fun tonight!"

Ted made the peace sign and the stranger walked out of the bar and raised his hands to the sky and said, "Thank you, Lord."

# XX

The high-pressure system over the Mojave Desert that had held the marine layer at bay finally gave in to the demands of "June Gloom" in San Diego. The moist, heavy air moved in quickly and consumed the sleepy little town of Point Loma, cooling it quickly from the heat that had ruled the last few days. Normally, Jack welcomed the mist. Tonight, it added to a dark and heavy mood that weighed on him. The conversation with Allie now played on a loop in his mind.

As Jack walked back to his boat to shower, he thought deeply. *I guess I've made no progress at all… It's been three years and I still feel the same, horrible guilt.* His stomach twisted into knots as he ruminated on the situation. "I'm always going to feel like this," he said aloud. He tried to remember what he felt like before it happened, but the feeling was elusive, and he couldn't conjure it up no matter how hard he tried. He considered blowing off their drinking engagement but knew that would leave him alone again with the box and the bottle; he lacked the courage to face either.

The mist had now blocked out the other side of La Playa Cove and cast a strange glow around the streetlights and dock lights. It felt cool on his dark tanned skin, weary of the sun that bathed it on most days. He wanted to just slip into the water. Swim to the bait dock, fellowship with the sea lions, keep swimming out past Point Loma and out to sea. He wanted to keep swimming until he reached Fiddler's Green.

Then he remembered the poem his great-grandfather had written, who had himself been a man of the sea.

*Long, so long have ye sailed the lonely sea,*
*To be committed to the deep when yer time it be,*
*But you've naught to fear from the dark-depth so mean,*
*For then you'll drink, dance, and sing upon Fiddler's Green.*

Fiddler's Green, the mythical place where women and men of the sea went to rest after they had served their wallets or a flag. It was a place of comfort for those that had led a hard, impoverished life. The myths and superstitions for the seafarer were maintained to see them through windless days, moonless nights, and terrifying storms. *Gloom and storms*, Jack thought to himself as he walked down his dock. He wondered if he would even be welcomed onto Fiddler's Green. Would they, too, see him as he saw himself? A shell of a man, a fraud, a coward, a complete and total failure? How was it that he could project the air of confidence for his guests, he wondered. What if they arrived at the dock and saw a shriveling coward, one that climbed into a bottle to hide? "I bet they wouldn't even get on the boat," he said to himself. Jack was spiraling downward.

He pressed all of it back, forcing himself to think of anything else. He hated this introspection and desperately wished to be more lighthearted, like Ted. Then he wondered, *is Ted lighthearted only because he is still young? Does age defile all of us?* To help stop the contemplation, he turned on Harry

142

Belafonte and let the thoughts of coconuts and the Caribbean wash over him. It was starting to work until *Jump In The Line* came on. He looked across the boat saloon and he could see her laughing, singing, and dancing to the music; it had been her favorite pick-me-up song.

"Damn," he said aloud and quickly switched to Led Zeppelin. The screeching vocals and guitars seemed to tear him away from the past as he finished getting dressed. He popped his ear buds in, called a car, and walked up to the street.

It was a short ride to downtown. The normally friendly captain was in no mood to chat with the driver, so the first time the driver said something, he just pointed to his ear buds and shook his head to indicate he couldn't hear her. She didn't take the clue.

"Are you meeting friends?" she asked.

"Yeah," Jack responded without elaborating.

"Have you ever been there before?" she asked while glancing back at him in the mirror.

"*Tequila Storm*? No, first time," Jack said as he thought, *Leave me alone.*

"Sounds fun! I'd like to go there sometime."

"My girlfriend says it's great - you should try it."

The girl smiled and nodded, then turned up the radio. Of course, he has a girlfriend, she thought to herself.

Jack thought, *I could have just asked her to join us, walked in with her on my arm. Blow it up with Allie, mind fuck Ted, ruin my relationships and friendships here, screw the Emo girl, and sail away in the morning. Break it all. Burn it down. Then, there is nothing to lose. No one to mourn because they hate me.*

"Jesus," he accidentally said aloud.

"I'm sorry sir, I didn't hear you," she said.

He played it off with a laugh, "Just talking to myself."

She smiled and turned the radio back up.

The car pulled up in front of the bar, and as Jack stepped out, he smiled and said, "Five stars and a good tip coming your way."

"Thank you!" She smiled at him.

As her eyes sparkled in a flash, he weighed it all again. Burn it down or build it up? He stood there staring in her eyes, ringed with dark mascara. His resolve built, and he said, "Drive safe out there."

Jack saw Allie and Ted standing at the bar and walked up to them. Before they could even say hello, he caught the bartender's eye and said, "Three shots, top shelf, dealer's choice." The bartender smiled and began taking bottles down off the top shelf.

"Well, thank you, Jack!" said Ted, but you know I don't drink, bro."

"All three of those are for me," he said

They laughed and Allie said, "I'm sure."

"No, I'm serious. I'm happy to buy you a shot or three, but those three are mine."

Allie had never seen that look on Jack's face before and it scared her.

"No, I'm fine," she said, "Just working on this lovely fresh strawberry margarita."

"You good, bro?" Ted asked with concern.

"I will be soon enough," he said as he glanced down at the first shot glass that had been set down in front of him. Without any toast or fanfare, he lifted it to his lips and drained it with ease. He set it down carefully, resisting the urge to throw it against the brick wall and watch it shatter into a hundred pieces. Anger was building inside of him. So much anger. He felt as if it might have the power to free him from the past if he would simply surrender to it.

*Burn it up, tear it down*, he again thought to himself.

The second glass was set down, lifted up, and drained just like the first.

"You're ridin' awful hard, cowboy," Ted said to Jack.

In a western drawl, Jack said, "Ted, there's a storm a comin'... A *Tequila Storm*." He motioned up to the sign.

As the bartender set the last of the three glasses down Jack said, "Three more, middle shelf, dealer's choice."

The bartender had seen it all before. He would slow him down if that time arrived, but he also could see a nice tip coming. Jack had just consumed $90 of tequila and was about to drink another $60. The bartender was doing the math, thirty-dollar tip in ten minutes - I love this job, he smiled back at his patron with a nod.

Allie put her arm on him, "Hey, Jack, you OK?"

"Look Allie, you can take me the way I am or take off, OK?"

He heard Ted's voice from his left side softly say, "Easy, Captain."

"Jesus, where did that come from? Who are you?" she demanded of him.

Another glass was emptied.

"This is who I am, Allie - and I've got nothin' to offer you or anyone else. I'm nothing more than recycled jokes, lies about myself, and a complete waste of human space."

"Jesus, Jack!" she said as her eyes teared up. She considered walking out of the bar as she fought the urge to cry.

Ted put his hand on him and turned him to face him.

"What the fuck, bro - you're over the line."

"You're funny, Ted!" he said sarcastically and laughed, turning to Allie. "This from the guy who talks regularly about doing it with my mom."

He looked back at Ted.

"I'm over the line? You, of all people, Ted, you have no right to talk to anybody about crossing lines."

The men faced each other and their eyes locked. The tension had built quickly to the point where it seemed the two captains might come to blows. Allie looked at Jack in complete shock.

Ted decided to try another approach, "Why do you think that captain wears that stupid striped shirt, Jack"?

The random nature of the question seemed to create a pause in his mind, forcing him to retrace his steps. *Things got heated. I flirted with the Emo girl. I saw Jen dancing to Jump in the Line. It was a good sunset. Ted's ridiculous outfit.* Then he traced it back to the root of his anger. *Allie made me talk about the past - that's why I'm mad…*

The three of them sat in silence as Jack stared at the fifth shot glass. He lifted it up, but this time he didn't drain it, he only took a sip and set it down. The ship was righting itself.

Jack said, "I taste oak, sweet agave - like a mother's milk…and something else…" He took another sip, looked up at the sky as if searching for the comparison or the words to describe the drink. "Cat piss. I taste cat piss."

He smiled and put an arm around each of them.

"He's back," said Ted as he glanced at Allie. "Jack?"

"Yes, Ted?"

"Would it be overstepping for me to ask - how do you know what cat piss tastes like?" Ted burst out in laughter at his own question.

Jack shook his head, and Allie looked down at the bar. She was still shaken by the eruption of the darkness inside of him. She wondered who he was, what he was capable of, and for the first time since she had known him, she wondered if it was safe to be around him.

"Guys, I think maybe I'll head home early," said Allie.

"Allie, I'm really sorry. Please stick around. I'll stay out of that dark room – I promise," Jack smiled softly and pleadingly.

"OK, Jack, but if I see even a hint of it, I'm bouncing."

"Fair," Jack said.

"Jack, Allie, for Christ's sake – could we focus?" Ted pleaded with them.

"On what?" asked Jack.

"The guy, the shirt, why, why, why!" Ted pounded his fist on the bar.

The two of them laughed at Ted, who was no longer trying to distract Jack; he was trying to solve a puzzle that was making his curious brain hurt.

"Set up two shots of the Reposado - one for my girlfriend and me, and a shot of tonic water for my friend here."

"Coming up," the bartender replied.

Ted would not be ignored.

"Well?" Ted asked.

"Well, what, Ted?" Jack asked.

"The guy, the shirt," then he interrupted himself, "Hey, I almost forgot…" Ted's voice trailed off as he reached his hand in the breast pocket of his shirt. He pulled out the forty dollars from the stranger at the bar earlier and waved it in the air, "Check this out; some guy who overheard my conversation in the head at The Pilot House comes up to me and asks if I know you. Turns out he's a friend of yours from Key West."

"No shit? What's his name?" Jack asked him.

Ted paused and considered the man's planned ruse, so he played along with a little white lie, "I totally forgot to ask - he just said 'tell him an old friend from Key West says hello.'"

"That's cool," said Allie.

"He laid these two Jacksons on me and said to buy you a drink."

"Why didn't he tell you his name?" said Allie.

Ted shrugged.

Jack felt like he had just been ripped from the room and wondered if Ted or Allie would notice that his mouth had suddenly gotten very dry. He could feel perspiration forming on his forehead.

Jack started to back away from the bar, "I gotta take a piss - maybe I'll call a friend from in there."

Ted and Allie laughed at the call back.

Jack turned and walked toward the bathroom while his mind began racing. He did have a lot of friends from his days in Key West. Why no name? Then of course, there was the one man he never wanted to see again. His mind flashed the image of him restrained by the military police in the hearing room as he lunged up at Jack like a rabid dog. He shook his head and said out loud to himself, "Don't go there, man."

On his way to the toilet, Jack was in an adrenaline induced state of tunnel vision. Taste, touch, smell, and sight were all laser focused on fight or flight just as nature had intended. With his mind preoccupied running scenarios, Jack walked past a man in a white Havana style button down shirt and Panama hat who looked like he belonged in an old Hollywood movie about the Florida Keys.

While the captain may not have seen the man, the man certainly saw the captain. In fact, his eyes had been solely on Jack Kelly the whole time. The man didn't see the happy people, the tight jeans showing the flesh below them with such clear detail, or tight shirts with muscles and nipples bulging, begging to be explored. He didn't see the three hundred tequila bottles, or the big chalkboard that read, *The hell with tomorrow, Tequila tonight*. The man only saw Jack Kelly.

"This was fun!" he said aloud after Jack had passed right next to him. He stood up and walked out the front door with as much attention as he had received when he snuck in from the alley. His car arrived quickly, and in ten minutes he was back at his hotel, which sat just above the docks where *Windborne* floated in her berth. His own head would rest on a pillow not one hundred yards from Jack's. If either he or Jack had known how close they would be that night, neither of them would have slept.

# XXI

Jack and Allie walked down to *Point Loma Eggz* and ordered their breakfast. Steaming black coffee was set down in front of them in well-worn china cups decorated with anchors.

"Keep that cup at high-tide, Jenny, I beg you," Jack said to the server.

"Anything for you, Jack."

Allie leaned over close to him as she walked away and said, "How many women in this town would sleep with you at the drop of a hat?"

"That's why I don't wear hats. Why are you talking so loudly?"

"I'm talking normal - your brain wiring is still all messed up from the tequila."

"Don't ever utter that word in my presence again, Allie."

"Tequila?"

"Yes."

"What if I sing it, like Margaritaville?"

"No."

"What if it's in a poem?"

"There's a poem about tequila?"

"Must be"

"Still no."

"What happened to Mr. Top Shelf?"

"He went too far down into the basement."

The server came back and topped off the coffee.

"Who do you think that guy was that bought the drinks?" she asked him.

"I dunno."

"Seems weird that he didn't leave his name."

"Yeah, weird."

"He said Key West - right?"

The thought of who it might have been was twisting up Jack's stomach in a knot, "Yeah - Allie, you are killing me with this morning talk show routine. Isn't there something more interesting than me on your phone?"

"Aye, aye sir."

She made a mock salute and pulled out her phone.

He wondered if the silence was actually worse than the pounding in his brain. He now heard everything around him: loud voices, plates slamming in the kitchen, the coffee pot banging on and off the hot plate, and Jenny shouting orders to the cook. As he sat there, his mind began to wander. He thought about all the people in Key West. *Maybe it was Freddy the rigger. Yeah, possibly that was Freddy - he always talked about giving San Diego a try. Or it could have been Juan, his Yanmar mechanic - his family was from Baja - maybe he came west for a visit? No, he thought, Juan would give his name. I hope it wasn't that coked-up nut-job Diego - he would do something like that.* But no matter how many names he forced into his mind; he couldn't force out the name of Jen's brother.

Allie was a quarter of the way through her plate before Jack even realized he had food in front of him.

"Nice to have you back; can I talk now?"

"Yeah - sorry Allie, I feel like crap."

"I didn't think you even drank that much"

"It gets worse as you age. It's like your body is pissed off at you for all the years of abuse. Like a bad marriage where your wife is holding it all in, and then on your twenty-fifth anniversary she calls you a pig and tells you to fuck-off."

"You paint a lovely picture of both biology and marriage. It's almost enough to make me want to become a nun."

"The nunnery wouldn't have you. Too irreverent. Too hot."

"Thank you… I think?"

"Don't mention it, dear."

"Nunnery isn't a word, Jack."

"Thank you, Captain," he said to her.

"Captain?" she asked, shocked by the title conferred.

"Captain Obvious."

"Walked into that one. Even hungover, the wit is still there, eh? It's cool, let me adjust my plate and flatware."

She started turning her plate and dropping it on the table while alternately banging her fork against it under the guise of rearranging it. The sounds pounded in Jack's head.

"You are pure evil, Allie."

"And that's why you love me."

She paused at her use of the word love and hoped she hadn't scared him.

"I mean, ya know, not LOVE, but like-love-like," she said humorously, to soften it a little.

He looked at her and sat silent for at least a minute. She glanced down at her plate and pretended to play with her food as she avoided his eyes.

"I do love you, Allie. Not like-love, or whatever you just said. I love-love you. I am in love with you, and it scares the hell out of me."

She resisted the urge to leap up and throw her arms around him. Slowly, she lifted her eyes to meet his and said, "Good. I'm glad you are finally being honest with me. I wasn't sure how much longer I could take of the strong and silent Captain Jack Kelly."

Now he looked down. He wasn't sure what to make of her response. As he thought about it, he offered, "I guess I had that coming, Allie. I'm really sorry about what I said at the bar last night, my head was in a pretty dark place."

"Yep, that was really uncomfortable Jack - please don't do it again," she said as she stood up.

They looked into each other's eyes and Jack nodded in acknowledgment of both his failure and commitment to do better.

"I have to go in early and help them prep for lunch - you OK with the bill?" she asked.

"Sure."

She turned and walked toward the door. He looked back down at his plate, wondering how he seemed to be continually screwing up the best thing that had happened to him in three years. Then, he heard his name and looked up to see her from across the room.

"Jack? Just so we are clear on this. I love you, too. I've loved you for a long time. Long before you asked me out. Probably long before I met you."

As she turned and walked away, the owner yelled, "Did you hear that everyone? She loves him!"

Jack shook his head in mock disgust at Vincent's antics, then yelled back, "Does that mean this pile of crap is free?" He pointed to his breakfast, and the restaurant erupted in laughter.

"It'll be free when one of two things happen: you run a fishing boat like a real man, or hell freezes over... And if I had to bet on the likelihood of those two, I'd buy some cold weather gear."

This time the crowd laughed even harder. The fishing boat captains banged their flatware against coffee cups. The din became almost unbearable to his hungover brain.

"I yield, I yield!" Jack shouted.

Everything began to settle down as the server came back to top him off again.

"She's a cutie, Jack, a little young for you, but cute."

He smiled at her and wondered why it was that women were always so quick to disapprove of a May-December relationship.

After he paid his bill, he made the short walk down to the docks, passing by a pelican that had made a semi-permanent home near the fish market. He was quite recognizable because there was a fishhook lodged in his bill. It hung there like a piercing he had bought at the local tattoo shop.

"Yeah, that's the right idea, mate," he said to the pelican. "Work smarter, not harder, let the fish come to you."

The bird eyed Jack with suspicion as he walked past.

Jack thought to himself that pelicans looked like mobsters. His mind began to drift away to an imaginary scene of pelicans with submachine guns and cigars in their mouths. They wore dark black fedoras with the brim pulled down low. As those thoughts passed through his mind, he began to hear the thumping bass line from *Another One Bites the Dust*. Just when it was all coming together as a musical, a familiar voice jarred him back to the present.

"Morning, Captain."

Jack looked up and saw Julie, the dock manager for *Sail this Bay*. As on most days, she wore a tropical print sun dress made from a stretch material that hugged every part of her curvy figure. Her long sandy blonde hair was pulled back in a ponytail. No makeup tarnished her face. He winked at her, "Jules - you could make any man cheat on any woman."

"Any man except you, Jack," she said with a smile.

"I'd be nothing but trouble that would ruin the carefree life you've built for yourself."

"You're running out of chances, Jack."

He smiled and asked her, "Wha'do I have today, mate?"

"Two couples and two singles."

"Roger that."

"Any anniversaries or proposals?"

"One proposal." She reached in the dock box and pulled out a banner. "The champagne is on ice in the cooler behind the nav station, and there are six glasses. The guy said he would like to offer a glass to all the guests. Oh, and he wants a special moment, so pick a nice spot and heave-to, Captain."

"Yes ma'am."

The captains all joked about how they had never witnessed a dock operations manager that bossed around captains the way she did. Not a single one of them ever said anything about it in her presence; they were all terrified of her and none of them knew why. At five-feet-two, one-hundred-ten pounds, she was not physically threatening. It was mainly her wit and ability to gut them like a fish with a few choice words. She knew it and they knew it; she ran the docks. They weren't really captains until the boat was untied from the dock, and even then, she was still the admiral.

He began his preparations on the boat below decks.

He heard Bradley's beaming, "Good Morning, Julie!" and Ted's "Hell, yes!" when he learned of the bridal party he would be entertaining for the next few hours.

"Ted!" Jack called.

"Ya, bro."

"Damn you and your *Tequila Storm*!"

He heard Bradley and Ted laugh.

"What's wrong?" Bradley mockingly and knowingly asked him, "Does someone have a booboo head?"

"Piss off, Bradley - you two are always the reason I end up feeling like this."

Ted's booming voice took the next volley, "Sounds like some serious denial, Jack. Maybe you have a drinking problem."

Bradley and Ted smiled at each other and chuckled like teenagers.

"I have a friend problem - not a drinking problem," he shouted back to them.

"Maybe you didn't drink enough, Jack," said Bradley. "Have you really considered that possibility?"

"Bradley, if I didn't know you so well, I'd say that was a sarcastic question," Jack said as he popped up from below decks. "However, since I do know that you can consume enormous amounts of beer, I will consider it a legitimate, scientific inquiry."

"Maybe we should conduct another experiment tonight," Ted offered sarcastically. "We could go back, you can drink the same amount, and then drink more. That way we can find out if Bradley is onto something here."

"You two are idiots. I hate you," Jack said.

"That's just the booze talking, Jack," Bradley said in a singsong reply.

Then, the sudden rattle of the authoritarian announcement from Julie, "Captains! The guests are starting to arrive - compose yourselves!"

"Yeah boss," Ted was the first to acknowledge her. He was followed by Bradley coming to attention to salute her, and Jack wrapping it up with, "You got it, Jules."

The men finished up their preparations and took their stations on the sides of their boats.

"Do you think we'll see him again today, Jack?" Ted asked in a serious tone.

"Who?"

"Captain Striped-Shirt," he said as he tugged on the torso of his own polo shirt.

A loud group of seagulls began fighting over a bag of chips. The three men stopped to stare in bewilderment at a bird flying off with a bag of nachos, as the other birds took off in pursuit. Jack said under his breath, "This could be a part of the musical."

"What's that, Jack?" Bradley asked.

"Nothing. Talking to myself again."

"Guys!" Ted demanded their attention again.

He was feigning annoyance over the interruption and stood with his hands out to his sides with the palms turned toward the blue sky.

"What?" Bradley asked as he shook his head.

"The guy, the shirt, what do you think?"

"Jack, if I may answer on behalf of the both of us?"

Jack smiled and nodded in approval to Bradley's question.

"Ted, how do I put this delicately," Bradley began. "We don't care, and we think you're insane," Bradley said with some degree of finality. Then he turned to Jack, "That was delicate, right?"

Jack and Bradley chuckled.

Ted yelled, "Now, both of you can fuck off!"

His voice had passed the threshold of what could be heard from the guest waiting area and Julie snapped at him, "Teddy!"

He held up his hands now with palms toward her to acknowledge his regret and surrender, as the three of them shook their heads and laughed at their own antics.

The guests were led down the docks by Julie in three groups. First, Ted's bridesmaid group was led on board. He wondered with anticipation about his prospects for a date that night. He would unabashedly say things that others might find offensive or outlandish. Today, with his group of bridesmaids, it would be no different. He could, would, and did say anything to anyone. It seemed that people either loved Ted or hated him, though Jack had never personally encountered the latter, and probably would not have cared for their company if he had.

Bradley's group came down much slower. The old man was ninety, it was his birthday. All he wanted was to be on a sailboat again - possibly for the last time. Bradley observed how the family adored him, and thought to himself, *He must have done something right in life.*

Finally, Jack's group was led down the ramp. One single was in front, then the two couples. The last man to board had on a ball cap pulled low, and large framed, very dark sunglasses. He seemed less friendly than the rest of the group, not making eye contact as he boarded. Jack didn't pay any attention to it. He saw all kinds on the boat: sane, drunk, sober, nice, mean, rude, caring, controlling, callous, excited, and fearful. Every few days he would run through the range of humanity.

It wasn't until the boat had reached the safe water buoy about an hour and a half later that the man in the sunglasses finally started to engage in the conversation with the rest of the group. Jack had noticed but didn't think much of it. As Jack prepared to tack the boat and round the buoy to head back into the bay, the man finally spoke in a complete sentence. It was a question to the captain, "Have you ever lost anyone, Captain?"

The guests laughed, thinking that he was making a joke. Jack responded to it as if the man wasn't serious, "Usually only one or two a week - I'm overdue now that you mention it."

The laughter made another chorus, like a choir singing along to the orchestra of flapping sails, a grinding winch, and sheets slapping on the deck for a few moments as the bow turned through the wind.

The man asked again, "No, seriously, have you ever lost someone while you were in command of a vessel?" His tone had become much more serious, which did not go unnoticed, as guests shifted in their seats and turned back to their own private conversations within the cockpit of the sailboat.

Jack continued to try to play it down, "Nah, don't worry mate - you'll be back on the dock before happy hour." He took his index finger and drew it in a cross over his heart. "Cross my heart and hope to die."

No one laughed this time.

"Not out here, I'm not asking if you've ever lost anyone out here, Captain."

There was something about the drawn-out manner in which he said captain that made Jack even more uncomfortable, and there was something familiar about the voice.

"Have you ever, anywhere, lost anyone?"

Jack was silent turning his attention to trimming the starboard sheet of the genoa. The man turned to the group, took off his sunglasses, and said, "I don't think our good captain is being completely honest with us," then looking at Jack, "Are you, Captain?"

Jack remained silent and stared at him as he recognized the face. The roar of the wind wasn't loud enough to overcome the silence. He could feel his stomach getting sick and the blood rushing from his head, and he felt dizzy. Jack held on to the wheel even tighter as he stared straight ahead without responding. Now he knew why the man had seemed familiar to him. He was Jen's brother. They had only met a few times. The first was when he and Jen had visited him in the hospital. The second was when he was released from the hospital, and Jack and Jen helped him find a place to live. The last time Jack had seen him was at the Coast Guard inquiry after the accident.

"Understandably, he doesn't like to speak about it - being that he was held responsible for the deaths of two individuals." Then he looked directly at Jack and said, "What did they call it again? Dereliction of duty?" Then he paused briefly before continuing, "His defense was rather pathetic; he referred to it as a lapse in judgement."

The man sat without saying more, while all of it sank in. The boat was now awkwardly quiet. Jack still said nothing. Finally, the young girl, soon to be engaged, spoke, "What happened, Captain?"

"I made a mistake - it resulted in two people losing their lives."

"And what steep price did you pay for that mistake, Jack? Did you have to forfeit your license? Jail time? Fines?"

"I had to surrender my license for a year."

"And what did you do during that year?"

"I worked the fishing fleets in Alaska, then sailed for a bit."

"That doesn't sound like punishment to me. What does this jury of your peers think - was that punishment enough to pay for two lives?"

"No," Jack answered the question that had been posed to the group. "There was no punishment that would have made it right - I live with it every day."

"Well, far be it from me to judge a humble penitent man - we all need redemption and salvation, Captain. Although I might suggest that if you are truly in so much pain, it is well disguised by the jokes, the tan, the lifestyle, the partying at *Tequila Storm*... it just doesn't appear . . ." he paused as he made eye contact with each person in the cockpit while making a face that evinced suspicion. "It just doesn't appear, to the untrained eye, that you suffer much at all." He shrugged and looked around at the group.

At this point, the young man who had intended to ask for his girlfriend's hand in marriage was now thinking he needed a new plan. He stood up and walked back to the helm. Leaning over toward Jack, he whispered, "Captain, let's not do the engagement thing out here, OK?" Jack simply nodded.

Jack's mind began to race. *I'm already starting to ruin more lives - this is never going to be behind me. It will follow me like the dark bloody stain it is. I will never be free of it. This will destroy me, Allie, even Ted or Bradley if they get too close to me. I'm cursed.*

"Maybe we shouldn't be too hard on him," the man said. "After all, we all make mistakes. Sometimes the payment for them is long-delayed." He stood up and walked toward Jack, who stayed glued to the wheel, his knuckles white. The man put his hand on Jack's shoulder in a gentle way as he turned toward the cockpit and stared at them for a moment. "I think this man's day in the sun is about to darken," was the last thing the man said, before he stood up, climbed out of the cockpit, and walked up to the bow of the boat. He acted as if nothing unusual had happened and sat down on the front of the sailboat to enjoy the view like any other tourist.

At the helm, Jack fought to regain any sense of control. He tried to focus on the basics: trim the sail, hold your line, watch that aircraft carrier coming out. While his mind was flooded with questions: *Why him? Why now? Jesus Christ in heaven - why now?*

The passengers had become like monks who had taken a vow of silence. There was an occasional exchange of a phone screen, but the tension in the air was palpable.

The last forty minutes from Point Loma to America's Cup Harbor seemed to go on forever. The sails came down without the usual jokes, stories, or tips on drinking and dining. *I just want it to be over*, Jack thought as he methodically finished his tasks. A sailor's routine was all he had to hold himself together at this point.

Jack put the boat in reverse and began the process of backing into the docks. He was normally focused, but not today. His muscle memory did most of the work in docking the boat, but it failed to account for the incoming flood tide pushing the boat sideways toward the dock. Crunch! The sound was a sickening mixture of splitting wood and cracking fiberglass. The boat lurched to a stop as Ted and Bradley who were already at the dock, rushed over to aid their friend as he sought to salvage his dignity. An event like this might normally have included a few friendly barbs - but both captains seemed to recognize that something was very wrong. Jack was never a very good poker player.

# XXII

After the second sail, he saw Allie coming down the ramp while he was cleaning up the boat and felt a wave of relief wash over him. She waved and smiled tentatively. Jack was too distracted by his own plight to notice that something wasn't quite right about her countenance. He stepped off the back of the sugar scoop and onto the dock after plugging the power cord into the boat.

"You are a sight for this sailor's sore eyes," he said, as he folded her tightly in his arms.

After the short embrace, she held onto his hand and looked up at him. He could see there was moisture in her eyes.

"What's wrong?"

"It's my dad, he's been diagnosed with cancer."

"Oh god, Allie, I'm so sorry." He hugged her tightly again.

"I'm flying up tonight."

"SFO?"

"Yeah. I've got a car on the way, I just wanted to catch you first before I left."

"Wow - this has really been a day for both of us."

"What happened?"

"It's a long story - I'll tell you when I see you again."

"I have a morning sail tomorrow, but I could fly up to meet you in the afternoon - unless you'd rather just be with your family."

"That'd be amazing, Jack. I didn't want to ask."

"You can always ask - anything," he said tenderly.

They held each other again, this time neither of them wanted to let go. Finally, she released him and said, "I gotta get to the airport. I'll text you their address - they're in Atherton."

"OK Allie. I love you."

"I love you, too." She hugged him again before turning away to walk up the ramp. She looked back at him and saw that his eyes followed her steps. She could see that he was distressed, and it was hard for her to keep walking away.

After she was out of earshot, he heard Ted call from his boat.

"She really does have a great ass, Jack - seriously bro."

"Filter, Ted, filter!" Bradley yelled from his boat.

The men sensed that something was off with Jack, and they looked at each other quizzically.

"Dinner?" Ted shouted to his companions.

"Absolutely!" Bradley shouted back enthusiastically.

"In," was all that Jack said.

As they often did when going out together, as one finished his own boat, he would help the next until all the boats were done. Then, the three of them would walk up the ramp together, place the *Sail this Bay* sandwich-board sign inside the gate, and check to see that the lock had engaged.

From the docks it was less than one hundred yards to the nearest barstool; and tonight, Jack was glad that it was no further.

# XXIII

The three captains faced each other in a horseshoe shaped booth and were thankful to be sitting down after two long sails.

"The guy with the ball cap that had a question mark on the front of it?" asked Bradley.

"Yeah, that's him," said Jack.

Ted said, "Whoa, that's the guy I ran into here who bought the drinks for us the other night - I had no idea, Jack. Obviously, I wouldn't have..."

Jack interrupted him, "Not your fault, little brother - this is all my shit coming right back out of the sewer and all over us."

Bradley weighed in, "Don't worry about us, Jack. And this isn't your fault. The guy is obviously an asshole."

"Well, no argument there - but he's a dangerous one and he thinks I killed his sister."

"Did you?" asked Ted.

"No, Ted, I didn't kill her. My decisions resulted in her death."

"What's the difference?" Ted continued.

"Filter Ted, filter!" Bradley smacked him with a folded napkin. "Ignore him, Jack."

"No, he's right. There really isn't any difference, is there my friend? I pick up a knife and stab you, that's murder. Decisions have consequences. I made decisions about who was on watch - maybe that was the cause of her death. The only reason I never spent any time behind bars is that they couldn't prove that my decision was the cause. Somehow it doesn't make me feel any better. Sometimes I wish they had locked me up."

"You can't live there, man." Ted said definitively. "What the hell happened out there, Jack?"

# XXIV

The man's name was William Davies, he was Jen's adopted brother. His had been a very hard life. His trials began at birth, and he knew it would continue until his days were done.

Jen's mother and father had been altruistic in their youth, and when they learned that foster parents were desperately needed for troubled teens, they took him in. With the passing of time, they began to question the beliefs they held. After the problems began with William, Jen had once heard her father say, "Maybe the cost is just too high for helping others." The toll William took on their family strained them to the point of breaking. As time wore on, the altruism of youth faded to the cynicism that can come with age.

William found their home to be very safe, and he was glad it was well-heated. He had lived in cold places that were not safe. He was so happy to finally be in a place where no one hit him or touched him. Jen's father called him "son," and that made him feel special, because no one had ever called him "son" before. He was determined to earn his place in their family, and he tried very hard. Despite his efforts, there were just things that he could not overcome: fear, anger, and sadness. They never arrived at once, but in waves that washed over him. Sometimes months would go by before his moods would change, but as he grew older, these events began to be more regular, and the effect on him became less predictable.

William was thirteen when he went to live with the Campbells. He had already been in and out of juvenile hall several times. Jen had been so sweet to him when he arrived; she did her best to make him feel like he was a part of the family. She was unselfish for a sixteen-year-old girl, and let him tag along on her adventures. Her friends tolerated it but were sometimes frightened by the way he looked at them. Her parents thought it was sweet that he was so protective of Jen, and for the most part, it had been harmless. Until one day, he saw a boy kiss her. It brought up emotion from deep inside him and made him remember all the times he had been touched, and he didn't want that boy or anyone else, to touch his sister. He sprung upon the boy like an angry bear, knocking him down to the ground and beating him so badly he had to be hospitalized.

Jen never looked at William the same way again. The boy that she had seen as troubled and harmless was now a monster - a monster that terrified her. William soon felt her change in demeanor, and he began to act out in fear and anger. He regretted those days now, but it had not been something he could control. Just before his fifteenth birthday, he was sentenced for the first of three times to a mental health facility.

William stared out the hotel window for what felt like an hour. He then looked down at the faded and folded picture of himself and Jen that he had carried for so many years. He noticed how the sides had chipped away, the creases from when it was folded in his pocket, the remnants of tape that had held it on the wall of his cells, and the color that seemed to be less real as each year passed. Looking up, he turned and stared into the hotel mirror hanging on the wall next to him and wasn't sure if he was the boy in the picture or the man in the mirror. At times, these extremes seemed almost impossible for him to differentiate.

"I miss you, Sis," he said to the photo. "I know that you loved him, but he's got to be made to pay a price. Everything has a cost. Remember, Dad always told us that choices have consequences and that we should make good choices. Jack made a bad choice and he's got to be held to account. It's not fair for him to be here and you to be gone. It's no different from back then, when they had to lock me up - I had to pay my price." He wiped a tear from the corner of his eye as he stammered on. "I'm sorry I missed your memorial - I was locked up again. I got into a sour mood after his trial, and I was deemed a threat to others or myself."

He paused for a long time and remembered the feeling each time he was processed into a lockdown: the cold feel of the linoleum under his bare feet, the smell of the antiseptic, the poking into places that were not supposed to be poked. He remembered the last time, when he had been so sad after her death, sitting on that cold steel bench naked and struggling to put on the hospital clothes that they had given him. He remembered that the man had tried to be nice - despite poking him - telling him, "You'll start to even out in a few weeks once the meds kick in. You just have to take it slow."

William sat and thought about all the medication. Everything seemed like slow motion at first and he recalled feeling so sad. He contrasted it to how he felt now without any medication; he could think about so many things at the same time - it all just seemed to come together so fast in his mind.

Then he shouted, "Yeah, I gotta stay off those MEDS!" he screamed loud enough to be heard in the hotel hallway by a family on their way out of the room next door to his.

"What was the name of the boat?" He had always struggled with words. The letters got jumbled sometimes, and it was hard for him to remember things that he saw. "Wind something?"

He continued the dialogue directed towards his deceased foster-sister, "Mom and Dad died. They were never the same after your death. Dad got cancer the same year. He found out when it was too late to do anything about it. Mom lasted another eleven months after that, but her soul had died with you. I remember looking at her eyes during Jack's trial; they looked dead, the light was gone. I think she held on for dad's sake, ya know?" He waited for an answer that never came. "I guess your captain really killed all three of you in some sense. Maybe he'll kill me too. Maybe that's what God wants."

William desperately wanted to know what God wanted. Sometimes he was certain, other times he felt so unsure, alone, and abandoned. That's how he felt now. He also felt that he had failed his sister, his foster parents, and God. His contemplation was a heavy weight that he bore alone.

He walked over to the phone and hit the button for in-room dining. He heard a man's voice on the other end of the line, "In-room dining, how may I help you?"

"I'd like another martini please."

"Same as before?"

"Yes, please."

"One martini to room two-twenty-four, will that be all?"

"Yes."

"Ten to fifteen minutes."

"Yes, and thank you," he said as he hung up the phone.

William set down the phone carefully and wiped it off with a handkerchief. He wasn't sure why he was wiping it off. He tried hard to remember everything that his mom and dad had taught him - Jen's mom and dad - but it was hard. There had been so many contradictions over the years between his many parental caretakers. Jen's parents were his fourth set of parents, and he started to think it through chronologically.

First, there was his biological parents. He didn't know much about them except that they had done a lot of drugs and had some run-ins with the law. They had taught him that it was alright if men visiting the house touched him. He remembered that he didn't like that. The courts finally deemed his parents to be unfit, and he was placed in foster care at five years of age. William wasn't sad he was being taken away from his parents and hoped he would be somewhere where he would feel safe.

William's first set of foster parents told him that it was not OK if anyone touched him. He liked hearing that but was also confused because of what his first parents had said. His foster mom was pretty nice to him, but the foster dad didn't seem to care much. He could remember him counting the kids like dollars at the dinner table. One time he overheard him say, "It's not as good of a deal as it used to be - takin' in these little fuckers." His foster mom had scolded him and said that he shouldn't swear, it was against God's will. William remembered that and he tried not to swear.

He stopped and thought about God again - why did God let all of these bad things happen to me? If he understood the Bible right, it was either because God loved him a great deal and was testing him, or because God hated him and was punishing him and he said aloud, "I can't figure it out, God."

He returned to the chronology. John and Mary, the second set of foster parents. They had seemed so nice at first, but then the touching began. He remembered what his real parents had said about it and thought maybe they had been right. He also remembered that it felt very wrong. He was eight by then. Once he protested and was beaten severely.

He spoke aloud again, "I never told you 'bout how bad it was in that home, Sis - it was awful."

He thought about the time that the state agent had asked him how things were going, and how he told them that it was, "very nice and fine." She seemed happy with his response, so did his foster parents. It was the house with John and Mary where he had his first "sad storm" as the social worker had called it. He was starting to experience what was determined to be clinical depression at nine. It was too much to bear for such a young and fragile boy. He remembered feeling so isolated and dark. It was just before his twelfth birthday when he stole a bottle of whiskey from the store. Since he didn't get caught, he felt emboldened, which led to the purse snatching, and that led to juvenile hall.

"Why did they call it a hall?" he said aloud.

William recalled how he had been so happy when his foster brother from his second home showed up in "juvie." He was sorry for Jeff that he was locked up, but happy to have a familiar face. Jeff had told him that he had been homeless for a year and celebrated his fifteenth birthday in an old VW bus in an abandoned lot with a guy that smoked crack.

His thoughts were interrupted by a knock on the door and the sound of a young woman's voice, "Room service."

"Just a minute, please and thank you," he said loudly. Then, softly he said, "I bet she's a pretty one," and then added "no touching," reminding himself of the rules.

He opened the door and stepped aside while the short, strawberry blond entered the room with a tray carefully balanced over her head, holding only one martini glass with three olives on a long skewer balanced against the side of the glass.

"On the credenza please and thank you."

"Yes, Mr. Davies."

She carefully lowered the tray without spilling a drop of the drink as the sweat on the side of the glass began to reach the napkin underneath it.

"Will that be all, sir?"

"Yes, please and thank you."

"Would you be so kind as to sign right here for me? The tip is included in the price, but you are welcome to add anything additional if you would like," she said as her blue eyes flashed up to him underneath the dark eyeliner.

"Why yes, of course young lady! Your service is impeccable! Here is something for you and the bartender to split."

"Wow, thank you so much - that is really generous."

She closed the ticket book, picked up the tray and walked out the door.

He could afford to be generous. Despite the disintegration of his foster relationship with the Campbells, they had set up a trust for William, in the hopes that it would keep him and others safe. The trust required him to have regular psychiatric care.

He picked up the glass and walked back to the window. He decided to stop the chronology for now, he didn't like the way it was making him feel. Staring out the window, he held up the glass to the boats that lined the waterfront walkway below him and said,

"Here's to you, Captain Jack - hope you've enjoyed your days in the sun. The dark awaits us both."

William drained the glass, ate the olives, and placed the tray with the empty glass in the hallway. Then, he said to himself, "Don't forget your tools," as he walked over to take something out of his suitcase. It seems like a lovely evening for hunting."

# XXV

Jack had drizzled it out to Ted and Bradley, like a movie trailer playing the highlights of the film on an endless loop in his own mind. The late-season call, the storm, the chaos. They were both ocean crossing sailors in their own right and had seen that kind of chaos up close. They listened quietly while he filled them in on bits and pieces of his life before Point Loma. After dinner, they said their goodbyes. Bradley slipped onto his bike, and Ted into his jeep. They waved at Jack, who had no intention of going back to his own boat.

Jack felt like he needed some time to think about everything again, as if one more time reliving it would absolve him of his guilt. He knew it was futile, yet he couldn't resist the urge. He walked back to the charter company docks, leaned on the railing, and looked out at the peaceful harbor that stood in sharp contrast to the storm inside of him.

Jack was deep in thought when he felt a hand on his shoulder and heard a familiar voice say, "Good evening, Captain."

He turned to see the face of William Davies, the man that upset the very foundations of his fragile new world. There was an evil smugness painted across his face. Then, Jack looked down and saw the knife. In his mind, the scene played out quickly: step right, sweep the arm away, control the knife, drive his fist into the man's jaw. But none of that happened. Jack just stood there as the man drew closer and placed the knife against his stomach.

"I had such a tremendous time on our sail today, Captain!"

Jack remained silent. His mind began running a new tape, *Just let it happen. Get all of this over once and for all. I deserve this. Just let it happen....*

"No comment from the great Captain Jack Kelly?"

"I never said I was great."

"No, well nonetheless, everyone just admires you so - isn't it odd?"

"Yeah, it's odd."

The man moved the knife up to Jack's throat.

"I've been instructed by God himself to exact vengeance. Do you have anything left to say for yourself?"

"No. Just get on with it."

"Suit yourself, Jack Kelly. This court, convened by the great Jesus Christ himself, finds you guilty, and sentences you to die by my hand, this day. Do you have any last words or confessions?"

"No, it's all been said before. I'm guilty."

"I'm glad to see that you are taking true responsibility here, Captain Jack. It will bring no mercy from me, but perhaps you'll find it in the next life."

William took a step back away from Jack and drew the knife up over his head. Jack was sure that he could see Jen's face reflected in the blade as it started to come down, he closed his eyes, at peace with his end.

All of a sudden, he heard Ted's voice and a commotion as he opened his eyes, Ted had the man in a chokehold from behind, and he had disarmed him. Jack just stood there and watched Ted constricting William's airway.

"Maybe I should just finish the guy, Jack."

Jack looked at Ted, visibly shocked at the offer.

"No, let him go."

"Come on, Jack? Are you nuts?"

"I'm serious Ted - let him go NOW!"

"Fine," Ted said indignantly.

Ted let the man slip to the ground as he picked up the knife and threw it in the water.

"We should call the cops, bro," said Ted.

"No. Let him walk."

"You're way off course on this, Jack!" Ted yelled back.

Jack had never heard Ted yell at anyone before and he tried to explain, "I know little brother - none of this makes any sense. I've got to follow my heart. I can't harm him. I simply can't. How can I hate him for wanting to do something to me that I've fantasized about doing to myself?"

"Well, you may not be so lucky next time, bro - I forgot to grab my backpack off the boat. If I hadn't, you'd be seagull food by now."

William was regaining his breath. He stood up awkwardly and looked at Ted and Jack. Jack spoke first, "I'm sorry for what happened to her and your parents - truly sorry."

William said nothing in response. Ted spoke next, "You don't belong here, dude. Get the hell out of our town or next time I might hold on to your throat a few seconds longer."

Ted walked up to William and looked up intently at him, "We clear on that?" Ted snapped.

William Davies nodded, turned, and walked away as quickly as he could.

Ted turned back to Jack, "I don't get it, Jack."

"I hope you never do, Ted – 'cause that would mean you'd lived it."

"Maybe I oughtta give you a lift back to your docks, Jack."

"Yeah, that would be good – thanks man."

Ted drove him the short ten minutes to the other side of the island. Neither of them said a word until Jack got out of the jeep.

"Owe ya one, Ted."

No jokes or laughter came from Ted this time. Only a faint smile and a nod.

# XXVI

Oddly, when Jack got back to the boat, he was hardly even shaken by the incident at the docks. He truly believed that he deserved to die for what he had done, or failed to do, and he was very much at peace with his conclusion. He had tried everything short of killing himself since her death; there was something about taking his own life that he could never work his way around; and he knew that Jen would not have blessed that course.

He began the nightly routine of laying out his tips, taking off his fish-hook necklace, then carefully placing the items along with his wallet and keys on an antique silver tray stamped USN. He picked up Steinbeck's *Cannery Row* and poured himself a scotch on the rocks. After bunching up some cushions on the settee, he kicked off his sandals, laid back, and began reading. Jack easily identified with the cast of characters in the novel, seeing their flaws and acknowledging his own. He read on as the group cooked up another scheme to get some cash but before he found out if they had met with success, he was fast asleep.

He awoke a few hours later to the sound of an errant halyard pinging against a mast somewhere nearby. He rubbed the sleep from his eyes and realized he still had to get his flight set up to join Allie and her parents. With a few clicks on his smartphone, he'd purchased the ticket and texted Allie with the details.

*How's it going with your dad?*

*He's strong - they've got a pretty good regimen in place for him.*

*I'm glad to hear that - I'm excited to meet the man that raised you.*

*Ahhhh,* was her only response.

There was a pause in the exchange as they both multitasked, Jack beginning to gather a few items for the trip, and Allie washing a few dishes.

*Jack, I may be bouncing up and down a lot while he's undergoing chemo - staying up here for extended periods of time - just wanted you to know.*

*Of course - you should do that.*

*Hell, we could sail your boat up if you wanted a place to escape.*

*:) Thank you Jack - I love you.*

*Love you too.*

He started a text with Julie.

*Jules - need a favor after the sail tomorrow.*

The response came about five minutes later.

*It's gonna cost ya Jack,* with a wink emoji.

*Name your price.*

*What'd ya need love?*

*Allie's dad has cancer. She flew out last night, and I'm flying up today to join her.*

*Can you clean and re-stock after my 10:00 AM?*

*Of course, Cap.*

*Definitely owe you - fish tacos when I get back?*

*I was thinking lobster is what you owe me at this point.* Another wink.

Jack glanced at the clock and calculated the nine hours of sleep he could get before his alarm went off at 7:00 a.m. Then, he brushed his teeth, pulled out his ditty bag and set it on the counter of the head so that he would remember to bring it with him in the morning. He threw a pair of khakis, underwear, and a few polos in his duffel bag, and laid Hemingway's *Islands in the Stream* next to his gear. After he finished packing, he took the book and walked back to the aft master. His mood had changed, and he no longer wanted to read about the exploits on *Cannery Row* - now he longed to be lost on an island.

Jack felt the emotional exhaustion as he folded into his berth. He opened the book, and within minutes he was on Bimini with Thomas Hudson and his children - it was the third time he had read it. It felt good to be back somewhere familiar. However, it was the wrong place for him to drift off to in his imagination. It was the last place on land he was with her before she died. Before he got through five pages, he was fast asleep and dreaming of a huge storm. Jen kept falling overboard, it was like a movie, and someone kept hitting play, pause, and rewind every few seconds. He would see her start to fall, then he would try to reach for her, but he was paralyzed. "Jen!" He would scream her name at the top of his lungs. Again, "Jen!" Except that this time, he felt the words coming out of his mouth in a twisted and garbled way and their sound startled him awake. He looked at the clock next to his berth. It read 1:59.

"Jesus, this is gonna be a long night," he said aloud, and then got up to piss. The nightmares were not new, but it had been a while since they were that intense. The day's events had painfully dredged all of it from deep inside.

Jack slipped back into the berth and drifted off to sleep again. This time it was Key West, they were on the docks, washing the boat. He could see her hair bouncing in the sunlight. It all felt so real. He woke up as he rolled over and looked at the clock again, it was now 3:11 a.m. He felt so sad, and his eyes were moist. He drifted back off, and this time he made it through until the sound of the alarm clock jolted him awake.

# XXVII

The morning sail was two-hours long. It was a route that generally meandered down along the San Diego waterfront to the Coronado bridge and back. On most days there was a fresh morning breeze, and the bay was still relatively empty at 10:00 a.m., so it made for a relaxing sail - even for a working captain. His guests for the morning were a young married couple on their first trip to San Diego.

"Where are you from?" he asked them.

"Nashville," said the woman named Shelly.

"Love that city," he said.

"Did you grow up out here?" asked the other woman, named Amanda.

"A bit north of here - Dana Point. If you've got a rental car, it's about an hour and a half and worth the trip."

"We do have a car - thanks for the tip, Cap'n."

He noticed her southern accent a little more as she said "Cap'n."

The other woman pointed up to the sail and asked, "How does it work? It doesn't look like we're being pushed."

"Actually, we're being pulled - it's lift, like an airplane wing. Do you see the curve in the sail?"

They nodded in interest as they considered the image.

"Just imagine it's like an airplane wing pointed up - the lift is being created by its shape. I control the sail's angle to the wind with this line." He pointed to the main sheet."

Amanda asked, "Can you sail directly into the wind?"

"Nope. The exact angle varies by the design of the boat. On this one we can get to about forty-five degrees off the direction of the wind."

He made a zig-zag motion with his hand moving toward the wind. "We tack the boat upwind by changing from one side to the other. Downwind points of sail are a little more of a push. There's some other stuff, like a keel under the boat that keeps us from slipping to the leeward - downwind - side of the boat."

"Cool," said Amanda.

Her wife looked at her and Jack and said, "Very cool."

They turned back to their own conversation and Jack drifted effortlessly out of the picture. It was a necessary skill for a charter captain to be there when wanted, and invisible when not. Jack's mind went back to the events of the day before. Ted risked his life to save me - I don't think I even thanked him. What's the guy going to do next? Do I have to look in every shadow, behind every door? Shit! He couldn't believe that it was happening now. It had all just started to come together. He felt as if he was trying to outrun his past and losing the race badly.

The sun glistened off the buildings downtown and the marine layer had retreated early, back to the edge of the peninsula. As the sailboat rounded the corner of Coronado Island, the guests found themselves staring up at an aircraft carrier tied off at what was known as the "carrier yard."

"That thing is huge - wow!" exclaimed Amanda.

The two women sat in awe of the mighty warship with its deck towering about sixty feet above the water.

"That's 71," said Jack as he pointed to the huge number visible to them. "Theodore Roosevelt - she's a Nimitz-Class nuclear powered carrier."

The girls turned back toward each other and kissed. Jack returned to his own thoughts. The morning breeze, and the upcoming trip out of town was making him feel a little less uneasy. He was growing weary of this in-and-out of uneasiness, guilt, and fear. Jack wanted all of it to end and didn't know how much longer he could keep going.

Shelly called him back to duty, "Can you take our picture with the city in the background?"

"Of course, pass me your phone," said the captain.

He turned the boat's angle so that the city could be framed up behind them without too much glare from the morning sun. Then, he leaned against the helm to hold the boat on course, and said "Alright, ladies, give me the runway model look with the wind in your hair."

The two young women laughed and played along as they made faces and poses for the camera. Then, he said, "OK, now one you can send to mom and dad."

They leaned in together cheek to cheek, and he snapped a few more pictures while tracking the approach angle of a harbor tour boat. He handed the phone back after a few more shots.

"You two look very happy and relaxed in those pictures," Jack said.

"We are. Thank you so much, Captain. We've been on this boat for an hour, and it feels like a day," said Shelly.

Her wife Amanda added, "This really is amazing."

Jack smiled and nodded. There was nothing more satisfying than seeing the effect that a short charter sail had on people whose lives were normally packed with corporate calendars, emails, and meetings. He had observed that the decompression was swift, and for some it was lasting.

The distance that would be traveled was always relative to the wind and current. This morning the wind was strong, and the current had started as slack, making the trip from America's Cup Harbor down toward the Coronado Bridge a quick one.

"Well ladies, this is about the turnaround point."

Amanda looked disappointed and asked, "Can we go under the bridge?"

The captain understood the question and its innocence because the bridge looked so close. "Speed, time, distance, wind and current," said Jack. "It seems like we are close enough, but in reality, that would put us back at the dock about thirty minutes late. The current is starting to turn against us as the tide floods in."

"Oh, bummer," said Shelly.

"Normally, I'd be happy to take you back late, but I'm headed to the airport to catch a plane to San Fran."

"That's cool, Captain, we understand," said Amanda.

"After I turn the boat around, you two should go kick back in the bean bag up on the bow." He pointed at the brightly colored bean bag on the forward deck.

"Ooohh, that sounds fun, can we take wine?" Shelly asked.

"It's yours to spill wherever you like," said Jack with a smile as they laughed at his joke.

The captain jibed the boat, bringing its stern through the wind as he brought the mainsheet in tight, and then began paying it out a little as the boat made the turn. He did this while bringing the head sail over for the new tack. With his hip placed firmly against the helm, he began pulling the line hand over hand and then wrapping it around the winch, he dropped the winch handle in and began cranking. His foot replaced his hip on the stainless-steel wheel, as he steered the boat onto its new course using only his foot. In a few moments it was complete, and they were headed back toward Shelter Island. Without saying a word, he nodded and pointed to the front of the boat, indicating that it was a good time for them to go up. They stayed on the bow for the rest of the sail.

The captain brought the boat into dock without hitting it this time and sent them off to get some famous fish tacos. Once they were gone, he gave Julie a quick hug and thanked her again. Then, he walked up to the street and opened an app to call a car.

The car arrived in a few minutes. The driver was Carrie, the same young woman that had driven him to *Tequila Storm*. She wasn't flirting this time but made easy conversation and he was glad for another distraction.

"Where you flying to?" she asked, after confirming his destination was the airport.

"San Francisco."

"Oh, I love it up there! I would move there but it's like three-thousand dollars a month to sleep in a closet!"

Jack nodded, "Yeah, it's hard to believe that there is anything worse than San Diego, but it makes it seem cheap to live here."

"I know right? It's crazy!" said Carrie.

"Yep."

They continued for the short five-minute drive from Shelter Island to the airport. Along the way, Jack looked at the boats docked along the back side of Harbor Island. He reminded himself of how much he loved this place, and then, he accidentally said aloud, "I wish you could have seen all this with me, Jen."

"Sorry, I didn't hear you," she said.

"Yeah, sorry, I was thinking out loud. I lost someone; she never saw this with me. It makes me sad sometimes."

"I'm sorry - well, I'm sure she's looking down smiling knowing that you are happy here."

"You're sweet - thank you. United, please."

She followed the signs to United and dropped him off.

"Five stars and a good tip," he said as he slid out of the car.

"Hope to see you again," said Carrie.

"Thanks," Jack said with a smile.

Jack made his way through security quickly as the crowds were light. He felt like a criminal fleeing the scene of a crime and began to run through the timeline. It's Sunday. Friday night had been the bar. Saturday was the sail with William. I can't believe that my life got so jacked-up in three days. What a shit show. I need to get out of here.

He looked around suspiciously, trying to pry beneath ball caps, hoodies, and sunglasses. I wonder if William is here; is he going to follow me to San Francisco? He realized he was being paranoid but couldn't shake the feeling.

"Now boarding United Airlines, flight four-two-nine at gate nineteen."

Twice he saw someone that he thought was Jen's brother. Finally, he was in his seat, looking out the window at the wing. "Two wings to take me to you, Allie," he said quietly to himself.

He pulled out the Hemingway novel and tucked it into the seat back pocket, along with his water bottle. Then, he sank into his seat and just stared out the window. *I wonder if thirty-thousand feet is high enough for me to get some perspective here...* he thought to himself as the plane taxied down the runway and accelerated toward the town of Point Loma. He looked out the window as the plane ascended high above Point Loma, over Ocean Beach, and out above the Pacific Ocean. He found himself straining to make out the tiny objects on the water. *Was that one a fishing boat,* he thought? *Caleb likes to fish that area, maybe that one is Caleb.* The thought of his friend fishing made him feel better as he took comfort in the familiar.

Eventually the plane made the turn to the north, and as it banked to the right, the wing tilted up and he lost his view of the water. He stared at the wing for a minute. Then, he looked across and ahead a few rows and noticed that he could see the other wing too as the plane banked to the right.

Lift, he thought to himself, as he observed the wing and recalled the earlier conversation with the ladies on his boat. He pictured the plane on its side, working like a sailboat wing. Jack Kelly had never been a particularly religious man, but he found himself saying a short prayer as the plane began to level off and continue its climb. *God, please let this feeling end.*

# San Francisco

# San Francisco

## I

The fog stood next to the magnificent Golden Gate Bridge like a mysterious and hungry traveler. It began biting into the peaks of its towers and then worked down to the base of the pilings until its appetite was finally satisfied; then it disappeared from Jack and Allie's view.

They had spent the day with her mom and dad, which had left them emotionally exhausted. They decided to venture out on their own for dinner, to give all of them a break. Now, they sat on the waterfront and looked out over the San Francisco Bay. Jack could feel the cold and damp on his skin, and deep in his soul as he struggled to find the words to tell her what had happened, and all that had come before it.

"So, the guy just dropped the bomb on you three miles offshore?" asked Allie.

"That's pretty much it," Jack said while shaking his head in disbelief.

She gently placed her hand on his right shoulder and made small circular motions, "I'm sorry, Babe."

"That's not the worst of it… he tried to kill me."

195

"Jesus in heaven, Jack! When, how?"

Jack recounted the events of the previous evening, Ted's heroic act and how Jack had insisted on letting him go free.

"I gotta say I'm with Teddy on this one. How could you just let him walk away after trying to stab you?"

"He's broken Allie, just like the rest of us. And, like me, he's got a huge hole in his heart. I can't blame him for wanting to kill me. I guess the upside is that I can't run from it anymore - it's all out in the open."

"Not for nothin', but you shoulda told me a long time ago. That's not the kind of burden that a man with friends should carry alone," she said softly and with compassion in her voice.

"I'm not good at that," he said with an air of regret.

"What part aren't you good at?"

"All of it. Letting people see who I really am. Admitting failure. Asking for help. All of it. I think that's why I idolize Ted so much - he's such an open book."

"It's not easy to let people in. I get it."

Her hand slid over to the side of his neck, and she pulled him in and gently kissed the side of his head.

"You loved her a lot, didn't you?"

"Jen? Yeah, I did. I hope that doesn't make you uncomfortable. I never thought I would feel that way about anyone again, until I met you. That's what scares the crap out of me - now I'm terrified of something happening to you. I feel responsible for keeping you safe."

"I love that quality of protectiveness, Jack; but you can't save everyone. And sometimes it's all you can do to save yourself."

The fog had decided to continue its feast of the San Francisco Bay. The Marin headlands were now gone, along with Alcatraz. It wasn't helping Jack's mood as he shivered to shake off the chilly June day.

"Twain was right," he said to her.

"The coldest summer I ever spent..." She trailed off as she quoted the reference.

He pointed over toward Crissy Field as he reminisced, "I used to windsurf off Crissy when I was younger."

"What were you doing up here, thought you were a So Cal boy?"

"I chased the wind for a few years after high school. Columbia River Gorge, the Delta, here."

"Did you go back and forth across the gate?"

"I did."

"I've heard stories about people losing the wind and getting sucked out with the tide."

"It happens. I've known guys who have overnighted on their boards in the fog and then come back in with the next flood tide."

"Sharks?"

"Big ones."

The foghorn reverberated in the distance as a car carrier floated eerily past them and disappeared from their view. Jack wished his past could disappear. Just slip into the fog, he thought.

"It was nice to meet your family today - wish the circumstances were different." He noticed her eyes teared up.

"He's a fighter. I'm really glad you're here, though. I love him so much, and this really hurts. You just don't see this coming."

"Life," he said with finality.

197

"Yeah."

"How about a hot bowl of clam chowder somewhere touristy and cheesy on Fisherman's Wharf?" he asked her.

Allie turned to look Jack directly in the eye, "Sounds good - but then you're gonna get it all out in the open - right?"

"Right." He leaned over and kissed her.

# II

Clam chowder in bowls made of fresh sourdough bread sounded comforting and warming, a respite from the cold and wet that surrounded them. The food was set on the table, and they quietly picked at the edges of the freshly baked sourdough bowl, with its piping hot contents. Their stomachs coiled like snakes, her present and his past both twisting inside them while they tried to eat the food. Jack took a long pull on the Anchor Steam beer and set the sweaty bottle down in front of him. He was still considering his options. *How do I tell her? Stay here with her and risk it all happening again?* He looked over at her amber-green eyes and knew that he couldn't walk away, he couldn't run from her. He pondered his fate. *Why is this dark cloud following me around?* He looked outside and saw only the dim glow from neon signs and streetlights which were close by. The fog now pressed in heavily, and he felt as if it was oppressing his soul.

Allie realized that she was halfway through her soup, and neither of them had said a word. She looked over at him with concern as he stared into the distance. She noticed the small scar on the left side of his chin, and the small creases around his eyes. *What are you thinking in there, Jack?* She wondered to herself. She picked up her hot tea and held the paper cup between her hands, enjoying its warmth.

Jack had torn off a section of his bread-bowl, piled butter on it, then dipped it into the chowder. His jaw worked hard on the chewy crust of the bread, while the rest of it melted warmly into his mouth. *Why do we have to do this?* He wondered. *Why can't it just be about today?* He knew when he asked the question that today would remain irrelevant until the ghosts of his past were vanquished. Those ghosts liked to hide in the dark places, free from the light of truth. He took another draw on his beer, this time longer than the first. He hoped that somewhere in that drink he would find the words to tell her the whole story without breaking down completely.

"We worked for a few years based out of Fort Lauderdale," he began without any introduction, picking up on the conversation that they had started over a month ago. "It's amazing how much you can earn and save when you work on a boat. Room and board are included, and if you don't blow your money partying in town..." he drifted off. "When we had a weekend off, we would try to pick up day work on charters. It was tough to find gigs at first, but then as you get to know people, you can work seven days a week if you want to."

He paused and took a few more bites of his chowder.

"In that time, we managed to save over a hundred and fifty thousand dollars. We started talking about our plan to buy a boat. What type of boat, what did we want to do with it, that kind of stuff. So, we put our heads down and worked even harder. By this point we had managed to break into the luxury charter circuit - those are the boats that charter for several hundred thousand a week - the tips are amazing."

He trailed off and took another long drink of his beer, wiping the sweat of the bottle off his hand before brushing it across the dampness in the corner of his eye.

"During our last summer in Fort Lauderdale, she started a class to train stewards, and I started doing freelance boat work. Our investment choices had paid off - a few lucky stock picks, and we managed to bank over three-hundred thousand, so we started shopping. *Windborne* was in Key West, she had been damaged in a storm, and absentee charter owners wanted out. Good timing for us. So, we packed up our bags and headed to Key West…" he put his left hand over his mouth as if the action could stop the words from coming out.

Allie watched his struggle, and while she had comforted him before, her instinct told her that this was a journey he had to take on his own. All she could do was listen to his story.

"I'll never forget that day we drove down there. The skies were clear, the turquoise waters all around as we drove over bridges and across the small keys. There was a place we stopped for lunch. Fresh barbecue gulf shrimp and beer on ice - I swear to you, it was the best beer and shrimp I ever had, Allie. It felt like my whole life was in front of me," Jack paused again to collect himself.

Allie sat patiently in silence and watched him search for the strength to speak the words. The words he had kept hidden in the box of pictures, those he spoke only when he was alone. She decided to help him gently.

"What happened at Key West?"

She watched his face as it transformed in front of her from a fearless man to a frightened boy. She wondered if it was really worth it - maybe this should be left unspoken. She was about to let him off the hook when he said, "Key West… that was where the end began."

# The Gulf Stream

# The Gulf Stream

## I

Four years earlier.

The bar sat on the waterfront above the harbor in Key West, a harbor that had long been the destination for those that sought escape. Palm trees, rum, trophy fish, sailboats, dive boats, and fishing boats - it was the picture of freedom and relaxation, and it was all contained within 7.2 square miles at the southernmost tip of the continental United States. The tiny key had also been the destination of other, less carefree endeavors over the centuries: pirates, slave ships, rum runners, drug runners, refugees, and commercial fishing fleets harvesting massive quantities of sponges and shrimp. The tiny paradise had wandered aimlessly through time like the palm trees that swayed above its shores.

With each passage of time and purpose, the city evolved and yet stayed the same, its sins hidden beneath its luster. The building that once housed the slave market became a sponge processor, which turned into a speakeasy, then a shrimp market, and now a bar - the Drunken Plank. A bar that welcomed the descendants of those whose freedom had been torn from them, now sold sponges in the gift shop, offered over a hundred types of rum, made you feel like a pirate, and cooked up the best giant gulf shrimp in town. Key West weaved its past artfully into its present.

The trophy fish were harder to find each year as the population on land continued to put undue pressure on the population of the sea. Charters could still be booked to relive Hemingway's life of sipping gin and smoking cigars while reeling in a majestic fish, it's majesty being the only crime to fit the punishment of the hook in its mouth. The Keys were a magnet for those longing for something else, anything else, rebels who spurned the traditional existence of a nine-to-five life punctuated with PTA meetings and Little League games. The same building that once held slaves now held those who sought to be free from society itself. They sat as friends, looking out at the swaying trees, while the trade winds washed away whatever remaining cares the rum had not.

Jack and Jen had been working very hard for the past two years, and Key West wrapped them in its linen as they slowly decompressed from the eighteen-hour days on charters and running their own side businesses. From where they sat on barstools, they could see *Windborne* resting in her slip with the U.S. Yacht Ensign waving gracefully in the fresh breeze. They sat with a college ruled composition book while sipping rum runners.

"You know, it's important that we get this on paper before the rum runners kick into gear. Right, Jack?" Jen smiled at the thought of the two of them penning a business plan while getting hammered in a bar.

"Don't you worry about me, Jen - I'm an Irishman through and through, and there is nothing, absolutely nothing, that I can't do drunk better than sober!"

"Nothing?" she said flirtatiously.

Jack said, "We don't have time for that now; let's start with a list of what we need to be ready for operations during the charter season."

They began with the to-do list: Coast Guard registration, website, taxpayer identification number… the list went on to become two columns on the first page of the new book.

"We're going to have to do some advertising to get going quickly. We can hit the hospitality circuit - hotels and resorts - to drop off pamphlets," he said to her. "Let's figure out a referral bonus for each booking. Maybe fifty bucks?"

She added it to the list and then took a long sip of rum.

"Why didn't we do this two years ago?" she asked.

"Two years ago, we wouldn't have been able to afford these drinks, remember?"

"How could I forget?" she said and kissed him on the cheek. "We could have just robbed a liquor store," Jen said as she made her right hand into a gun and blew the imaginary smoke from the barrel.

"Two weeks in the Keys and you're already infected - spoken like a true Key Westian," he said in an approvingly accusatory tone.

"That's not a word - don't make us look like dumb-asseses," she said to him in a mock condescending tone. The extra "es" on the word seemed to be a direct result of the rum runner kicking in. "It's Conch - as in, 'spoken like a true Conch.'"

"Close," Jack corrected her, "It's only Conch if you were born here, imports like us are Fresh Water Conchs."

"Jack, if you knew all that to begin with, why didn't you just say it?"

"Blame it on the rum," said Jack with a smile.

"We can sell those Conch Republic citizenships, too," Jen offered.

Jack laughed and said, "God, we are becoming depraved quickly in this place."

The list would not be finished that day. Jack and Jen had made the mistake of following the first rum runner with a second. The work would have to continue the next day, or the day after that. They had already started trading in their work ethic for an island attitude. Tomorrow is just as good as today - maybe better.

# II

Three years earlier.

Jack and Jen were now dream-makers and therapists. Their charter business had quickly gained notoriety, as an authentic experience and escape for anyone willing to part with ten-thousand dollars for a ten-day sail. They were not the least expensive small sailboat charter, nor did they want to be. One of the lessons learned in Fort Lauderdale was that the wealthy were willing to trade cash for relaxation - flush with the former and often destitute of the latter. The first year had been busy enough to allow them to spend the summer cruising Maine and Nova Scotia as they waited out the hurricane season. The second season had been even better than the first.

"I don't know about you, but I can't wait to boil those lobsters on the beach and swim in that cold water again," Jack said to Jen, as they were making a provisioning list for the passage north.

"Yeah, and I wanna hit that place in Camden with the lobster rolls - it was my fave!"

"Should we book any charter guests up north over the summer?" he asked her.

"I don't know. I feel like maybe I have one charter left in me - I'm beat. How 'bout you?"

"Same."

The cell phone on the saloon table started ringing and Jen answered, "*Windborne Escapes*, this is Jen, how may I help you relax?"

Jack saw her pick up a pen and her charter notebook, and he got the feeling that someone wanted to book. *It's too late*, he thought. He continued to listen as she answered questions.

"Yes, top shelf liquor is included," she paused to listen. "We do have dive gear, but you are welcome to bring your own." There was another pause while she considered the next question. "Yes, we can accommodate any type of diet." Finally, she said, "Can you hold on for a second while I confer with the Captain?" She made sure the phone was on mute, set it down on the table, and walked over to Jack with her notebook in hand.

"Well, skipper, looks like we can make a little more money if we want to do one last diving run to the Bahamas. The guy literally said, 'price is not an object'."

"I'm worried it's getting too late; I don't like some of the activity I'm seeing off the coast of Africa."

"We wouldn't have enough time to cross to Bimini, stay there for a few days, and then come back to Key West. Whatever that is off Africa will be getting too close if it continues to build."

He stopped and thought, and she could see him mulling over options. Her curiosity as to what they could charge above their standard rate of $10,000 per week was getting the best of her, "Just talk to him, Jack - maybe you can work something out."

"Yeah - no harm in having a conversation."

Jack walked across the teak and holly cabin sole to the brightly varnished table and picked up the phone.

"Captain Jack Kelly here. With whom do I have the pleasure of speaking?"

An Australian accent boomed back at him, "Hey, Cap'n my name is Dave Ryan."

"Nice to meet you, Dave. Here's the story. It's a bit late being June 10th and all, we're just getting ready to make our run north for the summer. Would you have any interest in making the sail north with us?"

"A bita offshore, eh mate? Wouldn't be poppin' my cherry - did that on an ARC," Dave said as the accent chopped off some words and merged together others.

Jack paused for a second and considered that since Dave had sailed in the Atlantic Rally for Cruisers, it might be nice to have another experienced, ocean crossing sailor on board for the sail north.

"You've been sailing for a bit?" the captain asked.

"Back since I was a shark biscuit."

"Shark… sorry, what?" Jack asked him.

"Shark biscuit - ankle biter - a kid."

Jack laughed at the euphemism and said, "The reason I ask, is that I can't make the trip to the Bahamas and back - there's some stuff brewing off Africa, and I want to get out of here while the gettin' is good."

Dave began again.

"I'd need to have at least a few days diving in the Bahamas - then I'd head north with ya. Could we make that work?"

Jack paused and considered the offer.

"It might be possible to do three days in the Bimini area. There are some great dive spots, like the Sapona, and Bimini Road - have you heard of that one?"

"Is that the fabled lost road to Atlantis?" asked Dave

"None other. Look Dave, I'm not trying to pressure you, but it depends on when you can get here - it would have to be pretty soon."

"No time at all mate - I'm in Miami today, and I can charter a heli and be down there in a few hours - we could shove off in the morning."

"Would it be just you?"

"No, my girlfriend Mallory, too."

"Then I guess that just leaves price."

"Name it and it's done, mate."

Jack paused, and then confidently said, "Twenty."

"I'll have Mallory email a list of our favorites while we're on our way to the heli pad. See you for dinner - cheers."

"Cheers," Jack replied.

The phone went dead, and Jack set it down on the table. He turned around to face Jen, cocked his head, smiled and said, "We're having company, dear."

"Did I hear you say twenty - as in thousand?"

"Yep."

"Wow, the Captain has some big balls!"

"That's a well-established fact, my dear girl. Let's grab lunch at the Drunken Plank one last time. But no rum runners today, we'll have to do a provisioning trip! His girlfriend, Mallory, is going to email us their favorites. We can hit the store after lunch. Cool?"

"Cool," she said as they high fived each other.

They wrapped up things quickly on the boat, now shifting back into work mode. Within a few minutes, they were walking up the ramp onto land, with large canvas bags slung over their shoulders. The bags would soon be filled with items which made for memorable sunsets and unforgettable dinners at anchor.

By the time they had finished a pile of gulf shrimp on top of a Caribbean slaw salad, they had the list from Mallory. Jen began to read it aloud, "Lobster and filet mignon, local fish - chef's choice, Caribbean jerk chicken and dirty rice, shrimp gumbo, Key Lime pie, Scotch eighteen-year-old or better, Tawny Port forty-year-old or better - we may have to rob the bank on the way to the liquor store!"

"I now hate the rule where we don't drink on charters!" Jack said with gusto.

They finished their lunch in the warm gulf breezes and paid their bill. As they stood up to leave, Jack said, "Hey, do you mind doing the provisioning run on your own? There is one other stop I need to make before we leave town."

"I don't mind, what do you need?"

"Can't say, it's a surprise for my girlfriend," he said as he leaned over and kissed her on top of her head.

"Ok, but it better not be one of those gifts for you parading as a gift for me!" Jen said sarcastically. "Like that massage wand? How was that a gift for me?"

"It made it easier for you to rub my back – that's a gift, right?"

She shook her head in mock displeasure, and kissed him on the lips, "It better be a good one since you're making me do this run on my own."

Jen secretly hoped that it was a ring; she had seen a card from a local jeweler sitting on his night table. *Don't get your hopes up*, she admonished herself as she headed to the grocery store.

Jack walked a few blocks down Front Street until he reached the jewelry store. He had managed to skim off ten-thousand dollars from tips over the last two seasons, to save for a wedding ring.

"Hey Damon," Jack called out as he entered the small shop.

"Captain Jack! Nice to see you – perfect timing!" Damon said as he reached below the counter and removed a small, black, box. "I think you are going to love it – more importantly, she will love it!"

Jack examined the ring carefully; the jeweler had created an exquisite wedding band well suited for a sailing woman. He had purchased a piece of gold from an old shipwreck, and had it made into a custom ring, decorated with nautical accents, sailboats, and a small diamond. On the inside of the ring, the inscription read, "I will love you always and forever."

# III

By the time they arrived in Bimini, the sun was just beginning to melt into the horizon behind them. Just ahead of them, was North Bimini, a strip of sand less than six-hundred feet wide in some places. This narrow, flat island is part of the barrier between the Straits of Florida to the west, and the Great Bahama Bank to the east. Its long finger extends north from its tip, connects to a wider section of land that turns east and then south, creating a deformed horseshoe shape. The Great Bahama Bank spreads out far to the east, with over a hundred miles of shallow water littered with shoals and reefs: a paradise for some, a nightmare for others.

The captain was always mindful on his approach to Bimini. He used his instruments carefully, and all of his senses as the water changed color quickly, receding from its thousand-foot-deep blue of the straits to the blue greens of the shallows. He noticed the way that the white sand bottom changed the reflection of the sun. It could seem warm and welcoming one minute, dark and disturbing the next. As with many things in life and this world, light changed the mood and sometimes the outcome. It was much easier to see hazards in the light.

In the last twenty minutes, Mallory and Dave had watched the sea change colors from the front of the boat as *Windborne* slid gracefully above the ocean floor sixteen-hundred feet below and then, suddenly, to one-hundred-foot depths. After that, the color of the water changed quickly as they approached the tiny island. Though the red and green channel markers were easy to see, the captain knew they did not always mark a safe path because the approach had shifting sand shoals.

"Dave, this entrance has some shoals, sometimes they work their way into the marked channel. Can you do a lookout on the bow for me?"

"Sounds good, mate," Dave said as he walked forward to the bowsprit and leaned out over the water.

Jack had enjoyed spending the day with Dave and Mallory. Dave was a venture capitalist, and Mallory an aspiring artist. This worked out well for both of them, because Dave loved art, and she could invest herself fully in it without a care for food, shelter, or spending money. He had underplayed his sailing experience a bit on the phone - which Jack had found typical of an experienced sailor. The ones with the real experience tended to be understated about it, and the captain appreciated that humility.

Jack had become fascinated with Bimini, and he often wondered what it must have been like in the 1930's when famous anglers flocked to the island in search of the massive fish that swam in the deep blue Gulf Stream. Long a fan of Hemingway, Jack often daydreamed about what it would have been like to sit on the fan tail of his boat and talk about life.

Queen's Highway ran up and down the small spit of land that contained everything Jack felt was needed in life: a good marina, decent restaurant, small store, and a bar. Potholes littered the road lined with old colonial buildings and brightly colored shacks.

Bimini was ready to welcome him once again as he had watched the depth finder change rapidly from one-hundred feet to fifty, to twenty, to fifteen. At fifteen feet the depth meter began to level off, occasionally dropping to twelve feet. Jack increased his focus.

"How are we looking, Dave?" Jack shouted.

"All good, mate," came the reply with a thumbs up.

Mallory and Jen popped up from down below with smiles; Mallory had a fresh Island Breeze cocktail in hand, one of Jen's specialties.

As they approached Bimini Blue Water Marina, Jack made a few last-minute mental calculations on the tide speed and wind. He eased the boat into neutral to check the speed of the flood current. Once he was satisfied, he let the boat continue to slow down, now being pushed only by the wind and current as it approached the narrow fairway on the left.

"I hate this approach on a flood," he said aloud.

"Dave, position yourself so you can get the stern line over that piling," Jack said as he pointed toward the dock.

"Aye, skipper."

Jack placed the mid-ship section of the boat within inches of the piling and watched as Dave tossed the line.

"Got it!" Dave shouted back to him, and then walked the line back to the stern cleat, tying it off.

Jack hit the bow thruster to push the front end of the boat toward the dock, while placing the engine in reverse to bring them to a stop. As the bow came up toward the dock, he could see Jen's toss was good and she was able to secure the bow to prevent it from being blown off the dock. Now that both lines were secure, he started barking orders.

"Jen, even out the bow and stern lines, and then secure fore and aft spring lines."

"Dave, if you need a little leverage on that stern line, just use this winch," the captain said as he pointed to the massive drum winch near where Dave was standing.

"Mallory, I'm putting you in charge of the beers for the crew! Go down and pull out three - and a near-beer for me." He never drank when they had guests, but he permitted Jen one beer at dock.

"Dave, if you can grab your passports, I'll walk down to customs and check us in."

"You got it, Cap'n," he boomed in his thick accent.

While everyone continued to scurry about fulfilling the captain's orders, he reached in the console on the cockpit and pulled out a small, yellow flag. The "Q" flag was used long ago to indicate sickness on board and warn others away. As he raised the flag, the others in the marina understood that it was no longer used to indicate sickness; now it was a desire to clear into customs. After he officially checked into the country, it would be replaced with the flag of the Bahamas.

Jack looked out across the small inlet where dark water pushed upward against an angry sky. The clouds began to roll in and he guessed that the barometer had started to drop. A single sailboat rested at anchor just outside the marked channel. Dave's voice shattered the moment of pure tranquility that Jack always felt after a long sail.

"Here ya go, skipper!" Dave said as he held out the two passports.

"Thank you, sir," the captain said with a smile.

Mallory appeared shortly after him with four sweaty bottles. Bottled beer was anathema to many on a boat. Jack hated canned beer and insisted that he could tell the difference. So, he took his chance with glass on the barefoot boat. His reason beyond the preference was that there was other glass on the boat, so why draw the line against a beer bottle? There was a glass jar of jam, a glass bottle of wine, and whiskey glasses emblazoned with the boat's name. He had endured several long-winded lectures from other boaters about the inherent dangers of glass. Some of those comments were from people who neglected to have their life raft re-certified before they left land. Everyone had their priorities.

Jack slid down the ladder quickly and reached in the dry bag hanging near the nav station, fishing out the two passports for Jen and himself that were in a small waterproof dive box. He put all four passports and the ship's papers into a well-worn canvas briefcase.

Jack said to Jen, "You know the drill, give 'em the briefing."

"Will do, Captain," and then she blew him a kiss.

The streets of Alice Town were still soaked from an earlier rain. Jack walked around huge puddles as he passed the brightly painted buildings marked with hastily made signs. Fish Today Fresh! $2 Beer. Bright blue, aqua green, and pale-yellow building walls rose up to metal roofs that looked like they would not survive the next big storm. As he passed a local bar, he could hear Bob Marley blaring out of the small, open front door.

The customs office visit was a matter of routine. The officers knew Jack and Jen well and had never had trouble with them or their guests.

"Hey, Captain Jack! You got da rum?" The officers laughed at their favorite joke.

"No, boss, I came here to get rum!" Jack answered as he handed them the passports.

"Good group on this charter, Captain?"

"Great couple - no worries in town, gents."

"We got no worries - just island breezes."

"That's why I come here; that, and the conversation with you boys," Jack said as he smiled at the men. "Is your daughter feeling better, Harry?"

"She's good as gold, Jack - thank you for askin'."

The officer handed the stamped passports back to him along with the other paperwork, and said, "Keep smiling, Captain Jack - we see you again this season?"

"Just when I check out in a few days. This is it for me, boys, heading north."

"Well 'den, carry on, Captain. Fair winds."

The captain smiled and waved goodbye to the officials as he made his way back out onto the street.

As he walked back to the boat, he thought about his present state of happiness. It had been such a hard reset after he and Dana broke up, almost like his life had ended and he was re-born. He had loved her deeply, and now he realized that he loved Jen even more. The thought terrified him and sent a shiver down his spine, even as the heat of the day released beads of sweat on his forehead.

The captain entered the small marina under the overhang proudly displaying its name, then along the docks and down to the end, where *Windborne* looked at home. Her occupants relaxed on deck and their laughter was the first thing he could hear as he approached.

"How is it possible for life to be this good?" he asked himself out loud, "Feels like I'm living in a dream."

Dave and Mallory decided they wanted to check out the Big Game Club for dinner, which left Jack and Jen alone for a while. Jack had decided that he wanted to propose to Jen on Bimini, because both of them loved it so much there.

"Hey, we're tied up at a dock and our guests are off the boat," said the captain. "Let's break the rules – I'm going to make you a Bahama Sunset."

"Sounds interesting, what's it like"?

"It's my version of a tequila sunrise, but with rum."

"Do you want me to make some snacks?" she asked.

"I want you to sit right there and relax," Jack said as he stood up. "I'll get everything together."

Mallory sat down and took in the beauty of the inlet as she waited for him to reappear. Ten minutes later, he started passing plates and glasses up to her.

"Hey, you're pretty good at this," she said teasingly. "Maybe we should switch jobs."

"Anytime you want. But we can't charge ten thousand a week if I am cooking them grilled cheese sandwiches."

"Point well taken."

The cocktails, with the humble appetizers, tasted heavenly against the backdrop of paradise. They engaged in light conversation, without a care in the world as they enjoyed the evening. After finishing the drinks, they sat mostly in silence and looked out over the water as the last few rays of light disappeared and the water grew increasingly dark. Jack flipped on the LED deck lights, which gave the boat a romantic air.

"Jen, I want you to know that since the day I met you, I dreamt of this day."

"What's so special about this day, Jack?"

Jack reached in his pocket as he stood up and walked around to the other side of the cockpit table. Then, he faced her, took her hand, and knelt down.

"Oh my god," she said.

"Jen, I love you more than life; will you marry me?"

"Yes, of course, yes!"

They heard Dave's voice, "What's all the commotion up here?" he said as he and Mallory approached the boat.

Jen leapt up, holding up her ring, and exclaimed, "We're getting married!"

"Aww, that's amazing!" Mallory shouted.

"Good on ya, mates!" Dave said with a huge smile. "How about a drink to celebrate?"

"Yeah, sounds good," said the captain.

The four of them left the boat, and walked over to the Big Game Club, where Dave bought drinks and desserts. Jack and Jen were beaming with joy. It was a feeling that would be short lived.

# IV

The three days diving at Bimini had been even better than Dave and Mallory had expected. Jack and Jen had used the time to continue the preparation of the boat, a job that is never-ending. On the morning of the fifth day, he began his planning for the trip north. He knew it was time to leave paradise, and an uneasy voice inside of him kept saying that he should have left yesterday. Even though Jack had made the trip before, he methodically rolled out the charts on the table showing the waters along the East Coast of America. Mallory was curious, and she stood near him, watching him pore over the charts, while Jen was preparing breakfast.

Jack looked at Mallory and pointed to Bimini, "We're down here."

Then he traced his finger along the map to an area offshore of Cape Hatteras.

"We are going this direction and further north to Boston." He pointed to the chart.

"We have plenty of deep blue water," Jack said as he outlined the area of open ocean on the chart, "so we don't need to worry about areas with reefs and shallows. There is a lot of commercial traffic in the straits - so we've got to keep an eye on our systems that track the big boats."

"Wow, I wish I knew how to do all that stuff," said Mallory.

Jack pointed over to the navigation station and said, "We'll train you and put you to work!"

The boat swayed at anchor as a morning breeze began to push against her sides. *Windborne* let out a soft groan as the tension held on the anchor snubber, and the line readjusted itself to the new position.

"Can I refresh your coffee?" Mallory asked him as he turned back toward the charts.

Before Jack could answer, Dave burst out of the head with a towel wrapped around his waist, still glistening from his shower. "G'day mates!" he said to the group, with Jack leaning over his charts and Mallory and Jen in the galley.

They turned toward Dave and Jen's jaw almost dropped. He was a very well-built man, and she had seen him in a bathing suit, but this dripping wet, towel wrapped Aussie momentarily stopped her in her tracks.

"Coffee?" Jen managed to say as she regained her composure.

"I'd love a cuppa if you don't mind, Jen."

Mallory turned to her to act as the interpreter.

"Tea, he means cup of tea."

"Good on ya," he said to Mallory. "Finally learnin' to speak proppa."

The group chuckled lightly.

"Wind looks good - should be south and east if the models are correct. They're light, but we've got the Gulf Stream for a nice push. I think we can still make over one-hundred miles a day. There are a few systems I'm watching, one that is far to the south and east, that should be fine. But there is a low developing to the north that I'll keep a close eye on. Unfortunately, it's where we need to go. The summer storms usually aren't too dramatic this time of year."

Jack began rolling the charts and moved them over to the nav station, as Jen began setting the table for breakfast. She had prepared coconut French toast with sausage patties, and fresh local fruit.

"Smells like heaven, love!" Dave's voice boomed from his berth as the toasted coconut aroma filled the saloon of the sailboat.

"Maybe something more formal than a towel is in order?" Mallory playfully suggested to Dave.

"Sorry mates, feel so at home I hardly noticed I wasn't dressed yet - be right back!"

The breakfast was soon set before them, and they began the discussion of watch-keeping for the rest of the trip.

"Nothing too complicated for the watches. Jen and I will cover the days. We'll be on autopilot unless someone wants to hand steer. At night, it's mostly taking a good look around you, watching the radar and AIS about every fifteen minutes or so. Other than that, it's logging our position, and occasionally trimming the sails."

"During the day, you are welcome to help, sleep, sunbathe, drink, relax, whatever you want. We'd appreciate your help for the night shifts if you are up to it; we'll run our first shift after dinner, 8:00-11:00, then 11:00-2:00, 2:00-5:00, and 5:00-8:00."

I'd like to help, too," Mallory said with enthusiasm.

"Yep," Dave said to confirm his participation.

"Great," Jack said. "I suggest that Mallory take the first shift as that is generally the easiest, since people are still up and about for most of it." She nodded in agreement.

"Then Dave, if you don't mind crashing early, you can take the second. That way if you and Mallory want to hang out a bit as your shifts overlap, it should work."

"It's all good, mate," Dave said in agreement.

"I'll take the third watch, and Jen will get the last watch: that lets her get a head start on some breakfast chores, too."

Mallory, taking this very seriously as it was her first formal role, asked the captain several more questions while Dave and Jen began talking about dogs. They worked their way through the food with great focus driven by the appetites built after days of sailing and diving. Soon the mountain of French toast was gone, along with every piece of sausage and fruit.

Jack looked at his watch, "Time to weigh-anchor and head out."

*Windborne* had anchored in a small, secluded cove. It had been such a peaceful night on board. Had the captain known that it would be his last peaceful night for many years, he might never have pulled the anchor out of that white Caribbean sand.

# V

Jack's dad had always said, "The best weather forecast is to just stick your head out the window." Jack knew that while the technology had improved, in essence his father was still right. They were three and a half days out of Bimini, and two-hundred miles offshore of Charleston, South Carolina, when he pulled the latest GRIB weather file from his satellite system. He sat down at the nav station with a cup of coffee, and carefully absorbed the information before him.

The ten-day forecast he had reviewed before leaving had been relatively benign, with the exception of a small low-pressure system about seventy miles offshore of Georgia. The file before him indicated something much worse. Temperatures had plummeted in the Northeast as the jet stream unexpectedly dipped down low in a horseshoe shape beginning over Wisconsin, then dropping down to North Carolina, before turning to the north and then up the East Coast. A rare summertime Nor'easter was forming about a hundred miles to their west. They wouldn't have time to make a run to shore which would require going through it, and if it continued to build it would be too large to outrun. Turning back might be an option, but that would mean facing the teeth of the Gulf Stream, as steep, closely spaced waves piled up from the opposing wind. The captain didn't like any of the options.

"Jen, a word please," he called up to her in the cockpit.

Jen came down into the saloon and walked over to his side while holding on to an overhead handrail. *Windborne* was still easily cutting through the chop that was building around them. The seas were becoming confused as winds started to build.

"Barometer's been dropping all morning. I just pulled this GRIB," he said in a serious tone.

She looked at the file and her eyes opened wide, "Where did this come from? Nothing was there a few days ago." Jen examined the image on the laptop screen. She noted the closely spaced isobars, wind arrows swirling counterclockwise, and a lot of red and yellow color indicating that those winds would be strong. She felt a little sick to her stomach.

Finally, Jack said, "It kind of looks like a Nor'easter - they are super rare this time of year."

"I'm going to pull a file to make sure there is nothing behind us. Go ahead and start making the preparations - here's the list."

Jack handed her the laminated list they had carefully developed with an old sailor in Key West. She looked at the rum stain on the corner, a tattooed reminder of its origin. It had been a warm, sunny afternoon when they sat in the Drunken Plank and talked about big seas with the old man. A veteran circumnavigator, he had rounded the capes in both directions, survived the edge of a hurricane, and even managed to live through a complete roll-over in the Roaring Forties, where the seas were always unforgiving.

She recalled his words as he gently patted her shoulder in a tender, fatherly manner, "Focus on the moment and what you can control - you'll be OK."

At the time, it had seemed like nothing more than a sensible precaution.

Jen couldn't believe that this was really happening. When they wrote the list, she never imagined that they would actually have to use it, especially not in the summer off the East Coast of the United States. She went on deck and called Dave and Mallory back to the cockpit.

"We're in for a bit of a blow," Jen began, "Mallory, why don't you go down and make sure everything in your cabin is secure, I'll be down in a few minutes." Then, looking at Dave, she said, "We need to reef - you've done this before?"

"Plenty and then some, love," Dave answered her.

"Pretty straightforward on *Windborne*, all lines are aft, reefpoints are marked on the line with black marker. I'll pay out the main halyard as you winch in the third reef line."

"Did I hear that right - reef-three?" He had crossed a few oceans, and realized that if she had not misspoken, this was bad news.

She pointed to the west, "It's not looking good. We'll do a full storm briefing once we get the sail in shape."

They could feel the wind had started to build. What had been picture perfect, deep blue waters just moments before, was now turning grey and threatening before their eyes.

Jen turned the helm until *Windborne* was at the optimal angle to the wind for reefing the sails. When she was satisfied with her angle, she engaged the autopilot, and they began shortening the main sail.

"Periodically, take up the slack on one and two as well so they don't bunch up," she yelled over the building wind.

After a few minutes, Dave gave Jen a thumbs up to let her know it was all the way down to the third reef point. Then, he locked the clutches and began coiling the lines to tidy up the area.

"Let's get the headsail reefed, too," she shouted over the building wind.

Dave worked his way back to the furling line that controlled the drum which rolled the massive sail in and out.

"That line isn't marked, but there are dots on the sail about a third of the way from the bottom." She pulled him over to her and pointed to the marks.

"Same as the main, you haul in and I'll pay out the working sheet," she said.

They began the process of reefing the roller furling sail. When they were done, Jen reset their course and reengaged the heavy, hydraulic autopilot that worked tirelessly below the deck of the sailboat. Then, she turned to Dave and looked intently in his eyes.

"Head on down below. You and Mallory can get your foulies on," she said, using the Aussie term for foul weather gear, "and your life jackets; I'll make up these lines and be down in a few minutes to start the briefing."

Dave nodded and went below as Jack was coming up on deck.

"How's the GRIB look to the south - behind us - any chance we can just run back to Bimini?"

"Our best bet now would be to bear off toward Ireland," he said sarcastically. "There's a tropical storm coming up behind us. We'd be nose into that wind and chop once we got south of this system." Then he motioned to the west, "There's going to be wind and chop from both directions - it's going to be a shit show out here. I think we're going to have to ride it out. I'm considering steering a bit further out to sea - maybe we can get to the edge of it. How's the prep going?"

Jen paused briefly after his question; the thought of going further out to sea terrified her. "Reefs are in, Dave is below suiting up with Mallory." She could feel the tension inside her building. Her mouth was getting dry, and she fought the urge to vomit.

"Thanks, Babe. Good work. You go suit up, too. I'm gonna make a sat call to the Coast Guard and let them know we're out here - see if they have an opinion on our direction. Then I'll call the marina back at Key West and ask them to start tracking the Yellow Brick." He was referring to the GPS position tracker on the boat. "I've shortened the transmission from four hours to thirty minutes."

Jen walked up and folded into his arms. He kissed her gently and pulled her in tightly to his chest. They were both scared. Neither of them had faced weather this serious. It was quickly becoming apparent that reading about conditions at sea could never fully prepare them for the reality. They quickly found the stark difference between knowledge, opinion, and actual experience.

Jen went below and stopped at the nav station to look at the second GRIB file to the south of them. Its closely spaced isobars and threatening red, orange, and yellow colors seemed to leap off the page at her. She looked closer and noted wind arrow barbs with three tails, indicating thirty knots. As she followed them around the cyclone, she saw some with a flagged tail, indicating fifty knots. Jen felt the nausea increase, along with a lightheaded feeling. She got her gear on, picked up the checklist, and carefully made her way to Dave and Mallory's cabin, using the handholds all around her to keep her upright. She began speaking to them with all the courage she could muster. "We'll start the briefing down here."

# VI

Thirty-six hours after the initial reefing, the headsail was now fully removed from the forestay to prevent the wind from putting too much force high up on the rig. The sails had been replaced with a storm trysail and storm jib. They were now on a four-hour watch rotation, with one person always available as a back-up to the helm. Jack had told them all in a tone of voice that left no room for questioning his command, "Above deck you are clipped in at all times - clear? No one ever leaves the cockpit unless they are clipped in, and I am on deck." With that, they had begun their shifts.

Resting while off duty on a sailboat in a storm provides little actual rest. The crew found it nearly impossible to sleep as the boat repeatedly slammed into waves, her rigging howling like tortured souls, and the occasional feeling of weightlessness underneath, after cresting a big wave and dropping down its face.

Mallory was faring the worst of the three of them and Jack realized that she would have to be taken off the watch schedule which would make it tougher for him, Dave, and Jen.

"Hey, Mal," he said to her in a soft tone. "I'm going to take you off the schedule - make yourself as comfortable as you can and let us know if you need anything."

Terrified, she nodded, through weary and teary eyes. The anger inside him, directed at himself, was already starting to build. It was his fault they were out here. His greed. His arrogance. He knew that if he and Jen had left when they intended, they would have been far enough north to duck into a port on the way up the coast. He questioned his ability to do this job, especially his ability to be responsible for peoples' lives.

Jack went up on deck to talk to Jen and Dave. He clipped in as he stepped out of the companionway. They looked wet and haggard. "OK," he said loudly, "we need to re-shuffle the watches; I pulled Mal from the rotation - she's toast." He had to shout to be heard above the storm, "Let's go three on, six off, round the clock." And then the command that would change his life forever, "One up, two down, we've got to get some rest, or we'll start making mistakes. We'll use the handheld boat comm system if you need help while on watch."

They nodded in agreement.

"I'll go first so you two can get a break. After me, Dave will go next, then Jen last. Get down below, dry off, eat, and sleep. The logs are already updated. The hatch stays closed behind you."

With that, the two of them moved toward the companionway, stepped in, unclipped their lifelines, and made their way down below.

"I'll make us something after we dry off," Jen said to Dave. "Check on Mal for me," she asked him.

Dave wearily nodded, as if the effort of processing her request was overloading his mind.

Jen looked around at the water that was accumulating on the cabin sole, then she pulled out three beach towels and spread them out below the companionway ladder. While taking off her foul weather gear, she had to wedge herself between the ladder and a counter to prevent her from being thrown to the floor. Even this simple task took its toll on her strength as the counterclockwise rotation of the Nor'easter was pushing the wind from the northwest and across the Gulf Stream at a ninety-degree angle. The seas were steep and confused. The boat hunted, but just couldn't find an angle to remain constant.

It was nine feet from the surface of the water to the top of *Windborne's* bimini sunshade. The wind generator sat another three feet above the bimini. Jen had already seen several waves before dark that appeared much higher than the generator; her best guess was that they were now close to twenty-feet high.

Jen hung up her gear in the wet locker at the bottom of the ladder and made her way over to the galley. Then, she pulled out some of the pre-made snacks she had prepared for the storm. They had covered the saloon table with non-stick shelf liner, and she set a few Tupperware containers on top of it. As an extra precaution to keep them from sliding, she wedged in kitchen towels around them.

Dave reappeared from his cabin, now in a workout tee-shirt and bathing suit. He was almost thrown into the starboard sitting area onto one of the permanently affixed swivel armchairs. Catching a handhold to keep him upright, he climbed arm over arm from one handhold to the next to reach the table. He slid in next to Jen and exhaled a sigh of relief.

"Not quite the quick summer getaway you had in mind?" she asked and somehow managed a smile.

"Maybe not - still beats sitting in another board meeting." He returned the smile.

"How's Mallory?"

"Green. Half asleep. Probably wishes she was dead."

"She might feel better above deck - but when it's this bad, the anxiety the storm will produce might make it worse," Jen said dryly.

She had begun opening the containers while speaking. Inside the first container, he saw bran muffins. His hand was inside the container, grabbing one so fast it almost hit her hand as she removed the lid.

"Sorry - I'm so hungry."

"No worries," she said in her best Aussie accent.

"Good on ya, mate," he said in approval of her slang.

The second container had pieces of fruit that were pre-cut into bite size chunks. They ate in silence as they sat side by side with the bare skin on their arms touching. They felt nothing sexual, nothing emotional, they were just two humans in a hostile environment. Touch and companionship were a gateway to comfort and hope.

"This is helping my stomach and my mind." He smiled at her. "You are an amazing cook, Jen."

"Thanks. There's a jug of cold coffee in the fridge if you want some when you wake. We won't do any hot meals until this is past – too easy for someone to get burned."

"Makes sense," he said as he nodded.


After they had finished, they cleaned up quickly and headed to their cabins, completely exhausted. As Jen laid down in her cabin, she pictured Jack standing at the helm alone.

"Radio check," she said as she held the small handheld.

"Radio check good," she heard Dave reply.

"Radio check copy," said the captain.

She thought about him again. She heard the resolve in his voice, but she also thought he sounded tired. She was thinking about him as she drifted off to an uneasy, nightmare-filled slumber, only made possible by her total exhaustion.

Up on deck, Jack stood watch while the others slept. He was in full foul weather gear, a PFD with a built-in harness, and a lifeline clipped to an eyebolt that went through the cockpit deck. The clips were positioned so that you could clip into one before leaving the cabin, and transfer easily to another at the helm, or to one of the long jacklines that ran the length of the boat from bow to stern.

Jack shook his head with his mouth open and uttered a sound as his head moved back and forth and his cheeks fluttered. The driving rain, along with saltwater spray as they crested waves, continually soaked him. Looking down at his watch, he wiped the water off the crystal and noted that he still had two and a half hours left. How is that possible, he wondered. "No more looking at the watch - when he comes out, he comes out," he said to himself out loud, fortifying his resolve.

The captain lost track of the passage of time. Fast? Slow? Moving? Stopped? He felt like he was at an intersection where everything was moving and yet stood still. He no longer felt tired; it was more of a numbness in his mind and body. He was hand steering the boat, keeping a balance between a compass heading, shifting winds, and building seas. It was a dance that would go on and on, a song that would seemingly never end.

Suddenly, Jack heard the roaring behind him and knew what was about to happen; a large wave was beginning to break, and it would swamp the stern and possibly the cockpit. He tugged on his lifeline to make sure it was secure, crouched behind the helm and held on while the water slammed onto the back of the boat. The captain tried to find the sweet spot on the helm as the boat began to slide down into the pitch-black trough of the massive wave. He steered a bit to starboard to take the boat down the wave's slope at a slight angle. What he couldn't see through the black night was that they were surfing down a fifty-foot wave.

After a few minutes, the wave rhythm and helm started to feel normal again. The captain peered out into the darkness, trying to see beyond the few feet that were visible, but it was impossible. The storm felt like it had reached its peak, and he was hopeful that the rest of it would pass over them by the morning. "We need to get through the night - this will be the worst of it," he said in an attempt to reassure himself.

Finally, he heard the Australian's voice boom out of the cockpit, "Mighty fine weather tonight, eh mate?" Dave chuckled as he said the words.

"Beats the hell out of a white sand beach and palm trees!" the captain shouted back.

Dave made his way back to the helm and clipped in. "Alright skipper, what's the heading?"

Jack reviewed the heading and gave Dave some guidance on the helm, "I know you've done this before - just don't over-steer when you're getting pushed by a wave. Small adjustments."

"Got it, Cap. Get some rest, mate. You look like hell." He clapped Jack on the shoulder.

Jack nodded and said no more as he unclipped and made his way below. It was midnight, and he had been up for twenty-hours; he was completely exhausted. Sliding out of his wet gear as quickly as possible, he reached into the refrigerator and grabbed a muffin which he devoured. He washed it down with a cup of water from the sink. Finally, after he made it to their cabin, Jack leaned over and gently kissed Jen as he crawled into their bed. She let out a soft, sweet sigh. It made him want to kiss her again, but before he could finish the thought, he was hard asleep.

A thunderous crash awoke the captain, and he found himself weightless for a split second before he slammed hard into the teak wall of his cabin. He and Jen found themselves tangled in each other as the boat reached a ninety-degree angle to the water.

"Brace!" he yelled, knowing that the boat would either roll or right itself, as sailboats do in these situations. Seconds later, the boat rolled mast down into the water and continued to roll until it came back upright. Jack and Jen were thrown from the wall to the cabin top as they were upside down, then briefly bounced off the opposite wall before being dumped back on their bed. Fortunately, *Windborne* was built for sea, and the cabin ceilings were low and padded for just this type of event.

Mallory's screaming could be heard from the onset of the knockdown, until the boat finally settled back upright in the water. Jack went into auto-mode as he heard the slamming on the hull that told him they had probably dismasted.

"Check on Dave. I'll check on Mallory and grab the emergency gear."

They were both disoriented. In a haze of adrenaline Jen walked right past her lifejacket and out onto the deck. The captain who normally saw everything, didn't even notice her mistake.

Jack saw a cabin strewn with food, plates, water bottles, towels, books, and electronics. There was a small amount of standing water beneath his feet that did not appear to be rising. Cushions, now separated from their settees, lay in a haphazard fashion around the saloon. Carefully stepping over and around the obstacles, he was on his way to Mallory's cabin when he heard Jen scream.

"He's gone - Jack, he's gone!"

Jack's mind was like a tunnel and everything else seemed out of focus. Gone? What does she mean gone? He tried to process the thought as he opened the door to Mallory's cabin, where he saw her huddled and crying.

"Hey - we're gonna make it. Are you OK?"

She tearfully stammered, "I think…I think so," with sobbing gasps between her words.

"OK, stay put until I come back."

Gone? He wondered again - Dave? His mind was starting to clear. "Christ," he said aloud as he walked to the nav station to hit the man-overboard button to mark their location. Then he saw that all of his navigation instruments were blank.

"Fuck me," Jack mumbled to himself.

He untied the Velcro on the emergency kit, cable cutter, and hacksaw strapped to the bulkhead next to the nav station and grabbed two head lamps with elastic straps from inside the cabinet. He turned his on and put on his PFD when he noticed Jen's was still hanging there. "What the…," he said as he picked her PFD along with the gear and headed on deck. He thought he heard Jen scream again, but decided it was the rigging which was groaning, creaking, and slamming against the backdrop of the storm's howl.

From the time Jack left his cabin, it had taken him less than ninety seconds to get on deck - it felt so much longer than that, like it was all happening in slow motion. With his arms full of gear and Jen's PFD, he shifted it all to his left arm and made his way up the ladder with his right hand, pressing his body hard into the ladder to prevent being knocked down. As he exited the hatch, the light from his headlamp eerily lit the empty cockpit area. The wind was still howling, but the rain had lightened. His mind was trying desperately to catch up to what he was seeing. Jen was not there. Dave was not there. He threw everything down and flung himself out on the deck of the cockpit, scrambling to stand up and find his balance. He felt his heart pounding in his chest so hard he could hear it and feel it in his ears. Where was she? He looked again, this time in every direction. Nothing. As he scanned forward, he could see that the massive mast had snapped and was now hanging by its remaining wire rigging, dangling like a sharp battering ram in the water, picking up its own hellish cadence… slam, slam, slam, as it pounded the hull without mercy.

His words started to form as if he had been in a nightmare and finally found the ability to scream, "JEN!"

There was no response. He clipped into the jacklines and scrambled low along the deck, up to the bow of the boat screaming repeatedly, "Jen!"

He made his way carefully back to the cockpit. The storm seemed to be lessening, as if its sole and final act had been to steal Jen and Dave. Now satisfied, it began to relax.

Jack threw the lighted, man-overboard buoy, grabbed the VHF mic and began the call.

"MAYDAY MAYDAY MAYDAY this is sailing vessel *Windborne*, over?" "MAYDAY MAYDAY MAYDAY this is sailing vessel *Windborne*, over?" "Anybody hear this, over?"

Then he realized that the top of the VHF antenna was on the top of the mast, which was now under water. He started yelling for Mallory and she soon appeared.

He put her in Jen's PFD, and said, "this stays on until I say so, OK?" She nodded tearfully in compliance.

"Where's Dave and Jen?"

"They're gone."

"What do you mean g-gone, Jack?" She stumbled through her words.

"They're out there somewhere, Mallory - we have to find them. But I need your help - can you help me?" he said to her plaintively, as he held both of her shoulders in his strong hands.

"Y-y-yeah, OK. What do you need?" She seemed to steel herself knowing that she had to function.

"Jen briefed you on the satellite phone, right?"

"Yes."

"Go get it - clip in when you come on deck - and point the antenna that way." He motioned with his hand to the south, then added, "The Coast Guard in Key West is pre-programmed. Grab the handheld VHF radio by the nav station."

As Mallory went below, Jack quickly scrambled to assess the damage. The deck and rigging were a mess. His mind tried to comprehend the force that it took to bend and break the strong stainless steel and aluminum components that now lay in a terrifying, tangled, and twisted mess.

As his headlamp managed to punch a hole into the dark water, Jack noticed that if he could get a line around the end of the mast, he might be able to change its angle so that it wouldn't punch a hole in the boat. That would give me the time needed to cut it away. "Worth a shot," he said aloud to himself as he worked his way back to the cockpit.

The captain's mind was running triage. I've gotta get that rig cut off before it rams a hole in the boat. Make sure the Coast Guard is clear on our situation. Get the lights on and spotlights out - maybe Dave or Jen will see us. Look at our track - try to determine which way they would have drifted - dammit, I can't look at the track - the instruments are off. Jen could be close. Dave - he must have unclipped for some reason - he could be close if he went overboard in the knockdown.

Mallory was back on deck with the sat phone. She was already dialing as Jack approached.

"Coast Guard?" she asked in a terrified voice.

A young woman with a strong, professional voice came over the phone, "United States Coast Guard Sector Key West, Petty Officer Harris, how may I help you today?"

"Help - this is a Mayday - here's the captain," said Mallory and then handed the phone over to Jack.

The young woman heard a more confident voice when Jack came on, but one still under extreme stress; she had heard that tone of voice before.

"This is Captain Jack Kelly, Sailing Vessel *Windborne*."

"This is Petty Officer Harris, go ahead, sir," she said with a southern accent.

"This is a Mayday. We have two crew overboard - whereabouts unknown." He paused, then continued, "The vessel was rolled, we have dismasted." He looked at the display on the sat phone which included his latitude and longitude.

"Our position is 35.19.136 north and 72.38.496 west." He repeated the position.

She read the coordinates back to him, and then began her questions.

"Is the vessel taking on water at this time?"

"I don't think so - we have some standing water below, but I think it was from the roll over."

"Are there any fires on the boat at this time?"

"No."

"Is anyone on board injured?"

"Minor injuries."

"When did you last see the crew that is overboard?"

"Dave Roberts was last seen at midnight; Jen Campbell was last seen five-ten minutes ago."

"Were they wearing PFD's?"

"He was, she wasn't."

"Did they have on PLBs?"

"Same - he did, she didn't. She left the saloon without her PFD and harness. God, I feel so helpless."

"I understand sir - let's stay focused here. I'd like you to activate the boat's Electronic Positioning Beacon so we can keep track of you, and I'd like you to call me back at this number - I'm not going anywhere until we get you secured?"

"Good copy," Jack said resolutely.

"Stay positive, sir. We are on our way to help you," she said in an energetic tone.

"Will do." Jack hung up the phone.

The Coast Guard immediately scrambled air crews and located the vessel closest to *Windborne's* position.

Mallory started to break down again, "Are they dead? Are we going to die?" she sobbed.

"No, Mallory, we are not going to die. I need you to hang on with me here - it's you and me now. We've got to pull it together, get this mast cut away, and try to find them." He put his arms on her shoulders again and then hugged her hard.

"OK. What do you want me to do?"

Jack began briefing Mallory; it felt like an impossible task ahead of them. But they knew that they were the only ones that could possibly save Jen and Dave, and that was a heavy burden to bear.

# VII

Mallory had lifted herself from the floor where she had lain, and risen above her fears, driven by the desire to find Dave and Jen, and ultimately her own desire to survive. She was clipped into the jackline kneeling over a mess of tangled rigging on a now hobbled sailboat hundreds of miles offshore. Mallory was holding on with all of her strength, while Jack cut and sawed.

"Almost there Mal!" Jack shouted. "Hold on a bit longer."

"OK," she replied.

The storm was lessening, making it possible for them to work on deck and cut away the rigging. Jack had deployed a sea anchor to keep them closer to where they rolled over - he was still hopeful he could find them.

The captain continued cutting, working his way through the twisted lines with the cable cutter, occasionally switching to a hack saw when the cutter was ineffective.

"Last one," he said as he snipped the remaining piece of standing rigging. Then, he untied the line he had rigged to keep the mast from pounding the hull, and let it slip away from the boat. He watched in exhaustion as the mast and rigging slipped quietly into the dark depths.

It had been two hours since the boat had rolled at 3:47 a.m., and the sky was beginning to turn a light grey as the day approached. The outline of the storm clouds was still visible in the pre-dawn light. Mallory slumped down onto the cockpit bench in complete enervation.

"I don't know what I would have done without you, Mallory," Jack said as he put his hand on her shoulder.

She instinctively moved in for comfort and pulled herself into his strong arms. They lingered for a moment before he pulled away from her warmth as duty came back into focus.

Jack went behind the helm, leaned down, and tried the engine. The first turn felt sluggish. The second turn sounded hopeful. "Come on old girl," he said in a coaxing tone. On the third try, the engine turned over. Jack felt a sense of deep relief as they had now regained control of the vessel. He left the boat in neutral for a few minutes while he cut away the sea anchor; he was too tired to attempt a recovery that would waste precious time they could be searching.

"We are unbelievably lucky that the Coast Guard cutter was so close to our position. Do you think they will be here soon?" Mallory asked him.

"I think they are about four hours out, but we can check in with them now."

He pulled up the speed dial on the satellite phone and pressed their number. He heard the phone ring once, twice, then the phone clicked and he heard the familiar voice say, "United States Coast Guard, this is Petty Officer Harris."

"I'm glad you're still there," he said.

"I insisted on staying at my post until our cutter was on station."

He updated her on their current position and status and asked about the arrival time of the cutter.

"Coast Guard vessel *Protector* should be at your position in three and a half hours."

"Copy that," said Jack. "We've finished cutting away the rigging and mast, the engine is running, and we are now in control of the vessel."

"I understand that the vessel is now under command; that's great news Captain."

Jack continued, "We are going to start a small grid pattern inside our horizon - maybe two miles?"

"Roger, sir. You are starting a two-mile grid."

"That's it for now Petty Officer; we have power again, so we'll leave the phone on. *Windborne* signing off."

"Roger, Captain. You call us if you need anything."

They ended the call. Jack turned to Mallory and said, "Three and a half hours 'til they get here - we're going to start a grid pattern now."

The captain turned the boat to the northeast and motored along slowly at five knots.

Jack said to Mallory, "In the cabinet to the right of the nav station, there is a big spotlight with a long cord, can you grab that for me?"

"Sure," said Mallory as she turned to go below.

Jack's mind continued to process the next steps. If Jen or Dave saw the light, perhaps they could try to signal him with their arms. Or the light might bounce off the reflective tape on the foul weather gear. He reached for something – anything – to hold on to hope.

It had stopped raining; Jack realized he was still suited up in his full foul weather gear and suddenly, he felt very hot. He reengaged the autopilot and started ripping his gear off as fast as he could. The sound of the metal lifeline unclipping, then the largest plastic snaps on the life vest, followed by a mix of Velcro and zippers sounded strangely loud in his ears, and he could feel his heart pounding. Finally, he was free of it. He felt lightheaded and had an irresistible urge to vomit. He launched himself out of the cockpit and headed toward the side of the boat to throw up into the water. He was not quite to the edge of the boat when the second wave of nausea washed over him, and he threw up violently. As he took another step toward the edge, he stepped in his own vomit and slipped sideways. Just as he fell hard on the teak deck, a stray wave quartered them from the rear on the opposite side of the boat, which was now devoid of its protective lifelines that were destroyed in the rollover. There was nothing left to stop him except the small, raised strip of teak at the edge. The momentum of the wave and his weight in motion was too great, and it rolled him sideways over the rail and into the water. He saw bubbles going up when he opened his eyes and kicked hard to follow them to the surface. The captain gasped for air as his head broke through the surface.

Jack was on the peak of a wave, and *Windborne* was in a trough, beginning to climb the next wave. "MALLORY!" he screamed as loudly as he could. She heard it just as she came back on board with the light. He screamed again, "MAL!"

Mallory followed the sound and saw him on the wave almost directly behind the boat, just as *Windborne* crested the swell and dropped into the next trough and Jack disappeared from her view.

"JACK!" she screamed.

The realization that she was now alone on the boat sent a wave of terror over her as she tried to figure out what to do next.

She had watched him turn the boat when they began the search and recalled how he had looked at the huge compass for a reciprocal heading. Mallory tugged on the wheel, but it wouldn't budge - the massive hydraulic autopilot was controlling the boat. She had no idea of how it worked, and her eyes scanned the instrument panel - most of which was blank - until she saw 'AUTOPILOT' and another button in red, labeled, 'STANDBY.' Mallory pushed the red button and immediately felt the helm respond and she continued turning until the boat was headed back into the direction from which it came.

Urgently scanning the water, Mallory fumbled with the cord of the searchlight and finally got it plugged in as *Windborne* crested a large wave. She pointed the light down into the dark trough and saw his silhouette, "JACK!"

He was waving his arms at her. The water looked murky, and the whole scene around her felt eerie and sent a shiver up her spine: the dark clouds, the dark water, and the spotlight which illuminated a ghost in the water. The boat lurched forward and picked up speed as it slid down the wave - it was headed right for Jack.

Mallory fought the helm, which seemed to have a mind of its own. As the boat slid down towards its Captain, she realized that she must have accidentally reengaged the autopilot, so she hit the 'STANDBY' button again. He was less than a boat length away when the helm answered her call, and she turned slightly to avoid hitting him. She had found the throttle, and pulled it back to neutral, then reverse - the way she had seen Jack do it when they had docked in Bimini harbor - then back to neutral as the boat slid up close enough for him to swim for it.

Now, even more terrified of falling off, she transferred her lanyard clip to the jackline and made her way over the aft deck to the scooped stern with the steps and swim ladder.

"Jack!" she screamed again.

He was there in a few strokes as he and the boat glided up and then down another smaller wave. She came as close as the length of the lanyard would allow. Jack had the swim ladder rigged so it could be deployed from the water. He dropped it down and using what little strength he had left, climbed back on board his boat.

He looked different than the man she had seen just minutes before. He no longer appeared to be a confident captain. Now, there was fear and desperation in his eyes. Jack saw the way she gawked at him, and it told him everything he needed to know about himself.

# VIII

Jack and Mallory sat in the cockpit huddled over coffee and a warm bowl of oatmeal she had made them as they continued their search. Jack took a slug of coffee, set the mug down, scanned the water around them and took a bite of oatmeal.

"The timing of the storm passing was luck," Jack said to Mallory. "I don't think we would have been able to get that mast cut away if the storm had been at its peak. You read about this stuff in books and think, 'no big deal, just a cable cutter and a hacksaw' but it's a lot harder in a confused sea, in the dark, when you're exhausted. You kept encouraging me, Mallory. I was so tired…," he looked at her and then rubbed his eyes with both hands.

They had been searching a grid pattern that the Coast Guard laid out after arriving. The Coast Guard cutter had sent a boat over to help secure *Windborne* and get all her systems operational. She had enough diesel remaining to run under her motor for seventy-two hours. Jack knew that at some point they would have to break off from the search and head to port.

Jack's resolve was weakening. A hole that would become deep and dark was opening inside him, waiting to swallow him up.

"We're not going to find them, Mallory."

"Don't say that, Jack!" she scolded him.

"She didn't even have a life jacket on, and - even if she did, it's no guarantee. Sometimes the goddamned things don't open and inflate!" Periodically he would feel rage, and it came without warning.

The color of the water had changed back to the deep blue hue that Jack had loved. Now he saw it like a temptress, inviting people into her beauty, and then springing the trap.

They felt their skin warming under the bright sky. On any other day cruising, this would be a day to remember. Blue sky, blue water, and a fresh breeze clearing the storm away.

"This is my fault," he said.

"How?" she asked with incredulity in her voice.

"I should have made better decisions - I should have seen this coming."

"You should have seen a storm coming? Jesus, the people we watch on TV get it wrong fifty percent of the time and it's their full-time job!"

"I should have slept on deck. Or maybe just headed out further east. I made the wrong choice and now they're dead."

She turned and hit him on the chest with both fists while she screamed at him, "Stop saying that, Jack! Stop it. Stop it. Stop it." And her eyes filled with tears again.

The continued release of adrenaline, the lack of sleep and emotional trauma had left them both raw.

"I'm sorry, Mallory."

He hugged her and leaned his hip against the helm to steer and then used the bezel on his watch to calculate his remaining fuel while considering the distances to the nearest ports.

"Mallory, we have to leave the search and head back to port; we'll run out of fuel if we stay much longer. Plus, I don't know how much longer the two of us will hold up."

Mallory nodded in solemn acceptance.

"Hailing Coast Guard Cutter *Protector, Protector, Protector,* this is *SV Windborne.*"

"This is US Coast Guard *Protector.* Go ahead, *Windborne.*"

"*Protector,* we are at our maximum fuel burn out here, and need to head into Norfolk. We'll notify Coast Guard upon arrival and advise of physical location and contact information. How copy?"

"Roger. Good copy *Windborne.* We will keep searching. Rest up and call us if you need us."

"Roger, *Protector* - and thank you all."

"Stay strong, Captain."

"Roger that, *Windborne* standing by on 16."

"*Protector* standing by on 16 and 22 alpha."

The voice at the other end of the radio had been caring and sympathetic. He wondered if the prosecutors would be so forgiving.

# IX

The months leading up to the trial had felt like a year, and the day of the trial had felt like the end of a lifetime. The first thing Jack Kelly had done after getting *Windborne* tied up at the dock was find a good, old-fashioned harbor bar, a place where the only expectations placed on the patrons was payment for drinks served. He sat on the same barstool from open to close and tried to buy enough alcohol to block out the memory of that night. A man who had never been given to routines was now governed by them. Bloody Marys until noon, beer until dinner, bourbon in the evening until closing. Then, stumbling back to the docks, stopping to piss anywhere he felt the urge, occasionally throwing up on the way. When he ate, he ate the same three things from the bar's limited menu: corned beef hash and eggs, tuna on toast, and the Harbormaster's burger and fries. The food had lost its taste and life had lost its meaning.

Mallory had decided to remain on *Windborne* because her life was now in disarray, and oddly, she felt safe there. One night, she was lying in her bed crying. Jack could hear her as he sat with a glass of whiskey just ten feet away - fighting back his own tears. Finally, he walked into her room and sat on the edge of her bed. She looked up at him plaintively. He put his strong hand on her face, and she took it in her hand and kissed it gently. Their need for comfort overcame any sense of loyalty to their recently departed loved ones, and they folded themselves into each

257

other, releasing pent up emotions, and feeling the joy of sexual climax. The next morning, she moved out of the boat, and Jack began drinking even more.

A few days before the trial, he tried to sober up a bit by slowing down the routine, but it was not until the day of the trial that he remained completely sober. He was now sober enough to feel, think, and worst of all, remember.

"All rise," said the bailiff.

The judge, a distinguished Coast Guard Commander named James Dalton, came into the courtroom, and brought the proceeding to order. Most of the trial remained a blur to Jack, who sat sober but completely numb and detached, focusing all of his efforts on blocking out the memories. As the day wore on, it was becoming clear that he would be held responsible and he began hoping that they would lock him in a deep, dark, hole. In his mind he was already there.

The final decision rang deafeningly in his mind.

"Captain Jack Kelly, this court finds you not guilty of manslaughter, but finds you guilty of dereliction of duty."

The judge glared at him.

"Sir, it was your responsibility to have a crew member on deck at all times, yet, you and your crew were sleeping while Dave Roberts, a guest, was on deck IN A STORM!" He pounded his fist against the bench. "Furthermore, while we deeply regret the loss of Jen Campbell, we would be remiss to not point out that she was not a licensed mariner; she should have been credentialed, Sir," he paused to let it sink in.

"It's charter operators like you, out to make the easy buck, sailing around and relaxing on white sandy beaches - it's operators like you that keep the Coast Guard busy. I have determined that as a sentence of this court, you will turn in your captain's license for one year. If at the end of that time, you are able to convince a panel to reinstate you, it will be considered. Until then, I suggest you get some professional help. You look like you are falling apart, and your local reputation in the bar precedes you, Captain." The judge said 'captain' with a certain amount of disdain. "This sentence would have been harsher if Lt. Commander Boyles from Key West had not spoken on your behalf. You would do well not to tarnish his character while you seem intent on destroying your own."

He turned to the non-commissioned officer at the side of the bench and said, "Bailiff, take this man's credential."

The Bailiff walked over to the table where Jack stood and waited for him to produce the passport-like document that contained his merchant mariner credential that listed his capacity as Master. As he handed over the red-orange colored book. Jack thought about how proud he had been when it had finally arrived in the mail. Getting that license had been one of the greatest accomplishments of his life, and it gave him a sense of freedom to chart his own course. On any other day, the thought of losing it would have been decimating, but at that moment, he didn't even care. All he could think about was getting back to that bar. The patrons at the bar didn't care who he was or what had happened to him, they didn't care if he carried a credential; they all had their own demons to contend with. Everyone that called that bar home had seen much better days. It was surrounded by the flotsam of failed careers, divorces, felonies, and sadness - all reasons in their minds to keep them on the stool.

He turned to his lawyer and said, "Well, thanks for trying, I know you didn't have much to work with."

His lawyer nodded, shook Captain Jack Kelly's hand, and watched the now suspended captain walk out of the courtroom and into an unknown future.

# SAN FRANCISCO

# San Francisco

## I

They sat on a bench shivering in the damp fog. The restaurant had closed an hour ago. Allie had been concerned that if they started the drive back to her parents' place, he would bottle it back up again, so she led him from the restaurant to a bench on the old wharf and let him keep talking. It almost seemed that he was unaware of his surroundings as he talked about everything.

"So, that was it. They took my ticket and put me on ice for a year. I went to her memorial service – her parents tried to forgive me, but they couldn't. They're good people, so they tried to hide their feelings of contempt. Who knows, maybe they were just reflecting back what I felt... what I feel about myself. I can't stop feeling it, Allie. It pollutes me. It's tearing down any good thing that comes into my life. It's going to tear us down – you and me." He intensely looked at her.

"We can't let it, Jack – you're not in this alone anymore; wherever you are, I'm there, too."

"I almost burnt it all down the night at the tequila bar, Allie."

"What d'you mean?"

"Some emo car driver was sending me very strong signals. I wasn't interested, but I thought, sure, why not? Break it all, tear it all down myself. That way, there's nothing to lose 'cause you've already pushed away everyone that cares about you..." he drifted off.

"That's an incredible level of self-destruction," she said with a tone of amazement in her voice. "And it's no way to live – hell, it's not really living, it's running from life."

He had been doing nothing but running and hiding since he left Norfolk. First to Alaska, then to the Marquesas, and finally to Point Loma.

"I kept thinking that if I went far enough, I'd eventually be free of the memory. No matter where I went, it was all still there. Tucked away neatly in that box of pictures, in my head, in my soul. Then, you came along. I never thought it would be more than a few dates or a fling - given our age difference - I figured you'd just move on."

"Jack, you can't outrun the past. No one can run that fast. Those three days in your entire life will only define you if you let them."

"I'm terrified of losing you or hurting you," Jack paused to let his words sink in.

"I've already signed on for all of it, Jack. And I love you more than I've ever loved anyone."

He moved his body back as the words hit him like a cannon.

"I love you too, Allie - that's why I'm terrified."

"Well," she paused, "let's be terrified together."

# II

Jack and Allie had been gone only two days, but it felt so much longer. It had been the break in the routine he had needed to help him slow down and think about how he felt. This morning feels different, he thought to himself. He still wasn't totally present, but instead of reliving the scene over and over again in his mind, he had started processing the loss. He didn't understand how, but it seemed that the combination of his confession and Allie's relentless love were laying a foundation that he could build upon. *I can't forgive myself yet*, he thought as the plane began to taxi down the runway.

"Sir, I need a verbal 'yes' from you, sir." The flight attendant said in an authoritative tone. "Are you willing and able to help in the event of an emergency?" she said again, in a somewhat annoyed tone of voice.

Jack felt an elbow in his ribs from Allie, bringing him back from the depths of his thoughts.

"Yes, I will," he said with a smile.

She smiled back and went to the other side of the aisle.

"I think we should leave for Hawaii soon. Maybe you need a good, long sail offshore to finish sorting it all out," Allie said to him.

"Yeah, let's get things wrapped up and toss the dock lines," he agreed with her.

He leaned over and kissed the top of her head. He loved her scent and breathed her in deeply.

The plane rocketed down the runway and lifted off gently as they were pushed back in their seats. She took his hand and closed her eyes. She said a short prayer to herself. *I hope I'm enough to keep you in the present Jack - I can't live with you in the past.*

# Shelter Island

# Shelter Island

# I

William Davies checked out of the hotel room that overlooked the boat which belonged to the man he blamed for his sister's death. His energy was gone. He could no longer hate Jack because he could no longer feel anything. In just twenty-four hours, he had gone from a feeling that he could conquer the world, to a feeling that his life was over. Such had been the dramatic and painful shifts for William.

He looked out again over the marina and saw all the boats. He thought about Jack Kelly again. *Captain! What a joke! That man isn't qualified to be the captain of a toy boat! Why did you take her from me, Jack? She was the only one that ever made me feel special.*

He methodically packed his bags, yet he wondered why he bothered. "Dad, do you remember how proud you were of me when I packed my first suitcase? You said I was a fine young man. I remember that, Dad. That was before I did all that other stuff and got in trouble. I wonder if you were disappointed in me. You never said, one way or the other. I wish you would have said it to me - man to man."

He sat down on the bed and began sobbing, saying over and over, "I miss you all so much."

As the sobbing began to slow down, he said, "I'm all alone now. I don't want to live all alone anymore."

With great effort, he forced himself up from the bed and walked over to the small writing desk. He set a legal pad down in front of him and wrote these words:

Jack Kelly,

I can never forgive you for taking my sister from me. You don't know all that I lived through before mom and dad took me in. You don't know how much it hurts inside to have no family to call your own. YOU DON'T KNOW!

I felt normal for a while. Even after I got put in the hospital for treatment, they were still my family. They came to visit me. At least I knew someone cared about me. Everyone cares about you, Jack Kelly - it's like the whole damn universe orbits around you. You don't care about anyone but yourself. If you had cared about my sister, you never would have taken her from me.

Well, I've fixed things so that you'll come to account for the steep price that others have paid for your actions - I've fixed things. You'll know, Jack - it's not about suntans and sailboats - it's about caring for people other than yourself.

You killed my Mom and Dad when you killed her. You killed all of us, Jack.

Live with that,

William Davies

He carefully folded the note into thirds and found a hotel envelope inside the desk. He placed the letter inside and wrote on the outside, *To: Jack Kelly*

William placed the envelope in his pocket, looked around the room one more time, extended the handle on his suitcase and wheeled it behind him as he left the room and went to the front desk to check out.

## II

Jack and Allie had landed in San Diego and were making their way through the airport. The bright reflection off the glass and steel was a sharp contrast to the cold June fog of San Francisco. They crossed over to the public transportation island and climbed into a car waiting on the curb.

"I feel really tense," he said.

"Why?"

"I don't know for sure - but I think it has something to do with her brother being here. It's like I'm waiting for him to pop out in a crowd and go, 'Look everyone! There's the man that killed my sister.'"

"Come on, Jack, do you really think he would do that?"

"He's already done it once on the boat - maybe a little more subtle - but the point was made. He wants people to know they can't trust me… Maybe he's right."

"He's not right - you're a good captain, you're just a shitty deity."

His head snapped around at her, "What?"

"Jack - you're not God. You don't control it."

He sat back in his seat and let it sink in while Allie gazed out the window at the rows of boats lining the inside of Harbor Island. Within a few minutes they were turning onto Shelter Island Drive.

"Maybe I should hop out here - closer to my boat," she said.

"No. Stay with me, Allie. I don't like the thought of being alone right now."

She smiled and leaned into his shoulder.

They heard the driver say, "What is all this about?"

Jack and Allie looked over the dashboard and through the window, down the narrow, two-lane road. They saw flashing lights across from one of the boat yards as the traffic continued to pile up in front of them.

"Accident?" Allie asked.

"At 11:15 a.m. on a Tuesday on Shelter Island?" Jack replied.

"Idiots drive around the clock, Jack."

The driver laughed.

"Look, friend," Jack said, "we're a short walk from here. No point in you sitting in this for twenty minutes. You can turn right there - it will take you back to Point Loma."

"Thank you!" said the driver with a big smile.

They got out of the car and began the short walk down Shelter Island to *Windborne*. Jack noticed that the morning north-westerlies were starting to fill in as he watched the palm trees swaying gracefully in the morning breeze. The marine layer had already begun its retreat over Point Loma, and he could see the small ripples forming on the water beneath the fuel station at the Shelter Island Yacht Basin adjacent to La Playa Cove.

Jack could feel the gentle sea breeze on his face washing over him. It brought him comfort thinking of the wind coming and going as it pleased.

"How can it be so comforting and then so devastating?" he asked out loud, almost forgetting that Allie was beside him.

"What?" she asked.

"The wind. It's making me feel so good now - but I've seen what it can do. I've stared into its teeth."

"I'm glad you're feeling better - stay in this moment - stop thinking about the teeth of the wind. For this moment, the wind is your grace."

"Yeah - I feel it. You're right… as usual." He winked at her.

"As long as we can keep that part of it straight - the part about me always being right - we'll have a long and healthy relationship," Allie said as she playfully slapped his shoulder.

As they walked along, they noticed that a crowd was gathered, and they saw Bradley and Ted staring toward the scene.

"Yo - *Sail this Bay*!" Jack shouted at them.

The two men turned around upon hearing the name of their charter company and waved him over.

"What's going on?" Jack asked.

Ted, looking very disturbed, simply pointed without saying a word. Jack's head turned quickly as it followed the direction of Ted's arm and extended out from his pointing finger toward the old, big fish scale at *The Big Reel Club*. Its steel arch stood fifteen feet high and twenty feet wide, with hooks for attaching big game fish. As he surveyed the scene, his brain was having a hard time processing what he saw.

There was a fire truck with its ladder extended, reaching out toward the top of the arch. He saw two firemen pulling something off one of the hooks. It was the body of a man.

"It's the same guy, Jack," said Ted. "I saw it happen and I tried to save him. It happened too fast. He dropped hard and it snapped his neck."

"Christ! Ted - I'm so sorry. This is all my fault..." his voice trailed off as his eyes remained locked on the scene in front of him.

Allie could see Jack's progress slipping away right before her eyes. It was visible on his face; she could feel the change in his energy. She imagined him running down the docks toward *Windborne*, jumping on the boat, and pointing it south and west - never to be heard from again. She pictured herself running after him, trying to hold on to him.

One of the Harbor Police officers who knew Jack saw him and walked over.

"Hey Captain, mind if I have a quick word with you?"

She didn't wait for an answer as she gently took his elbow and guided him away from the crowd.

Allie turned to Ted.

"What the hell is that about, Ted. Did you say something to the cops?"

Her accusatory tone stunned the man who considered her a friend. Bradley, always the peacemaker, broke in.

"Easy Allie, Ted said nothing, I was right here with him when the cops arrived. All he told them was that he saw it happen and tried to help."

"Sorry, Ted. The last couple of days... My dad has cancer, and I finally got Jack to tell me the whole story. It felt like he was really making progress. Now this. Fuck."

"Fuck indeed, Allie," Ted said gravely.

When the officer had Jack out of earshot to the group, she said, "Did you know this guy, Jack?"

"Sort of."

"How sort of?"

"He was the brother of a woman I was engaged to a few years back."

"Where's that woman now?"

"Dead."

"How?"

"Storm at sea - under my command."

"That explains the note." She reached in her metal note folio and took out the envelope with Jack's name on it.

"What's that?" Jack asked.

"Suicide note - want to read it?"

"No - I'm sure I know what it says."

"Sorry to have to break that to you, Jack."

She turned to walk back towards the body, then stopped and turned back toward Jack, who stood frozen and staring off into the hundreds of masts and fly bridges on the water below him.

"Jack?"

"Yeah?"

"He says he fixed it so that you'll have to give an 'account' for what you have done," she said, making air quotes around the word account.

"Any idea what he means by that?"

"No idea. The Coast Guard tried and convicted me. I lost my license for a year, but manslaughter charges were never filed by the DA. I'm surprised he killed himself and not me."

"We ran his background - in and out of institutions all of his life, almost never violent. Except one time he nearly beat a kid to death - something involving his sister," the officer told him.

"Yeah, she told me about that time. She was terrified of him after that happened."

"Just be careful, Jack. You never know with people that are detached. Maybe he set something in motion, or maybe it was all in his mind. You never know for sure - they don't even know for sure."

"Thank you," said Jack.

He stood and stared, fixed on the distance while thoughts began ravaging his mind. *Another one dead on your watch, Captain - when will you finally realize you are nothing but a danger to others. Maybe I should have killed myself and spared everyone else more of my misery.*

He felt Allie's hand and turned. She wiped the tears from his cheeks gently and took the strong man into her arms. She knew he was broken, and she saw past it to his future.

# III

After walking from the scene of the suicide to the dock where *Windborne* rested peacefully, it was hard for him to grasp the sharp contrast. *How is it that it can be so tranquil here, when a few hundred yards away, it's complete chaos?* His mind was racing with so many thoughts. *Maybe I can't handle any of this. If I was on an island in the middle of an ocean, I couldn't destroy other people's lives…*

"Jack!" It was the second time she had called his name while tugging on his arm, and he was so deep in his own thoughts that he hadn't even heard her.

"Sorry," he said in a quiet and defeated tone.

Allie suggested, "Maybe we should go down to the park at the end of the island and just hang out for a while - how's that sound?"

He paused and thought about it. "Thanks for the offer, but not today. Would you mind if I peeled off on my own?"

Allie was taken aback by the question. Just moments before, he had implored her to stay with him. Now her mind churned on the reality of what stood before her; a broken man intent on being alone in a time of crisis. She struggled with her next words, "Uh…yeah, sure, whatever you need to do, Jack."

They walked a few feet further, and with each step, Allie's confidence drained out of her. Now she felt a knot in her stomach, and she could feel her heart pounding in her chest. She didn't want to intrude, but she felt compelled to know.

"What are you planning on doing? Just hanging out at the boat?"

"No," was all that he said in response, not answering her first question.

*Please don't make me ask you again*, she thought to herself as they walked along the waterfront.

"I've got something that I need to do... I've needed to do it for a long time."

"OK, Jack, I'll see you later."

He barely stopped to give her a kiss.

Allie could almost feel the cold stone of the wall he was quickly erecting around himself. She remained silent as he walked away.

# IV

Jack wasn't at the boat long before it left the dock. He backed *Windborne* out of her slip and reminded himself that his "home" could be picked up and moved to anywhere in the world just that easy. He liked it that way.

The captain carefully eased the boat down the fairway and into the small inlet of La Playa Cove. *The water is so peaceful at this time of day*, he thought. He looked around him at all of his favorite sights: the hills, the marinas, the sea birds, and the sun glistening on the water. Jack turned up into the wind. Methodically, he slowed to idle and put the boat on autopilot. He stepped around the helm and took three wraps of the main halyard around the winch, and then hit the button that controlled it. The lines groaned loudly over the electric motor as the sail came out of its stack pack. He continued looking around him for any obstacles as he finished setting the sail. Finally, the captain trimmed it for a beam reach and walked back to the helm, turning off the autopilot and switching off the engine. It was the same feeling every time the motor switched off; instantly he began to feel it all melt away. *This is where I need to be… stop fighting it.*

# V

Allie felt sick as the surge of adrenaline worked its way through her body. She picked up her pace, doing what she could to run out the clock on the "fight or flight" response. As she neared the end of Shelter Island, she decided to stop off at the docks of *Sail this Bay*. The gate was open as they prepared for the afternoon sailing charters. She could see Bradley and Ted going about their chores.

She stood on the dock where both captains could hear her.

"Hey, boys," she called out to them.

Both of the men stopped and looked up, smiling when they saw her. Ted hopped off first and walked over to her, "How is he?"

"I wish I knew - but I think he's not in a good place."

"Shit," was all that Ted said in response.

Bradley approached and gave her a quick hug.

Ted looked at him directly as he spoke, "We may have a problem with our friend."

Bradley nodded in a knowing way, looked at Allie and asked, "What happened after you guys left?"

"He just started to shut down. It was like that night at *Tequila Storm*, but not as harsh. This time it was like… resolve."

"Where is he now?" asked Ted.

"I don't know - maybe at the boat. He wouldn't say what he was doing or where he was going. He said that he had something he's needed to do for a long time. Guys, my stomach is in knots."

She started crying.

Bradley put his arms around her in silence, and Ted broke it, "He'll pull through this - I have a lot of faith in him. We all do."

Allie answered him with hesitation, "I don't know if I'm built for this roller coaster, guys. I mean, I really love him, but, this sucks."

"Yeah, it does," Bradley said as he looked down at the dock.

Ted nodded. His compassionate gaze was louder than words.

Julie could see this was a tough moment as she walked down the ramp, but they had boats to sail, and the guests were congregating at the top of the ramp.

"Hey guys - sorry to butt in…" She trailed off as she nodded her head toward the gathering crowd above them.

"Roger," Ted acknowledged her.

Bradley gave Allie another hard squeeze, "I'll be back in three hours - text me if you need me."

"Yeah. Thanks, guys."

Allie turned and walked up the ramp, doing her best to compose herself before walking through a dozen strangers. She squeezed through the crowd and avoided making any eye contact. The walk to her own marina, which she had made so many times, felt awkward and uncomfortable. The feeling inside her was choking her, making it hard for her to breathe. She realized she was in the midst of a full-blown panic attack, and sat down on the bench just above *Sail this Bay's* docks.

She hadn't been aware of how much time had passed when Julie put a hand on her shoulder, "Hey, Allie. Are you holding up OK?"

"No. I'm unravelling."

Julie was older, and her life experience had included plenty of pain and loss. She sat down on the bench next to Allie and put her arm around her. "Allie, Jack Kelly is a very complicated man. He's also got a heart of gold, and he's as loyal a friend as you will ever know. If you can ride this out a bit longer, I think you two will find the other side of it."

"Thanks Julie. I don't know if I can do it."

"I understand; just do the best you can," Julie said as she stood up and put an arm under Allie. "Ok, up you go, let's walk down to your boat."

The two of them made the short walk down to Allie's marina where Julie said goodbye and then headed back to the office.

Allie was now alone, and she was breaking.

# VI

Just a few miles away from Allie, *Windborne* slid gracefully through the water past the tip of Point Loma. The pain that Jack had felt just an hour before, seemed to be nearly gone as he breathed in new life from the salty air. He had taken boats out past this point hundreds of times and usually dreamt of the islands that lay before him out there somewhere. Islands he missed and longed to see again. He had never considered that the desire to be somewhere else might suggest cowardice, rather than an adventurous spirit. The boat pushed on, as if she were a willing accomplice in this act. The captain hand-steered until he was about six miles offshore, and then he flipped on the autopilot.

Jack left the cockpit and went below. He saw the box on the shelf and began to think about William Davies. He had hated William just hours ago. Now he felt sadness and compassion, along with a strange sense of loss for a man he never really knew. William had been the last living connection to the woman he had loved. He thought about those islands to the west and south of him: Hawaii, Marquesas, Tuamotus, Tahiti. His own voice almost startled him as he broke the silence, "I can't keep running, Jen - I have to let you go. I'm sorry I let you down - I'm sorry I've been such a coward since you've been gone. I know that none of it is what you would have wanted for me. I think I can finally accept all of it, Jen. I will always love you, but I've got to let you go."

Jack waited for a response that would never come. After a few minutes of sitting in silence, he picked up the box and set it on the table. He opened the liquor cabinet and took out the bottle of rum and two of the ship's crystal glasses. Then, opening the box, Jack saw his favorite picture of the two of them together; they stood smiling, standing in front of *Windborne*, stern-tied to the dock in Key West. He took it out and set it down on the table.

"I remember when you ordered these glasses - you said we would be running a classy charter." He poured a little rum in both glasses. "You made it happen, we did run a classy charter. Those were the happiest days of my life. I miss them, but I know I can't live there anymore."

The two glasses sat on the table next to the box, and he put away the bottle in the cabinet. He walked over to the utility closet where he kept tools and supplies. Reaching in, he felt around for an old piece of waxed canvas cloth that he'd had since he was in the Boy Scouts. Next, he went over to the fishing tackle box and pulled out some large weights. His last stop was his rigging bag, where he retrieved some waxed whipping twine.

Walking back over to the table, he carefully unfolded the canvas on the table. Picking up the box, he set it down in the center of the canvas and placed the weights around the sides of the box. Jack began folding the canvas around the box until it was completely wrapped up. He placed the rigging twine underneath it, and then tied it in both directions so that it would remain closed.

The captain picked up the two glasses in one hand, and the box in the other. With his hands full, he leaned on the ladder and reached up with the box to set it in the cockpit, then the glasses. Then he climbed out, picking everything up as he came into the cockpit.

The captain walked slowly to the back of his boat and unclipped the lifeline that allowed him to walk onto the sugar scoop stern and sat down with his feet in the water. Jack looked at the package one more time while he contemplated the weight of what he was about to do. He knew that there was no going back, it couldn't be undone. He held up one of the glasses in a toast.

"Here's to you, my love, I hope to see you at Fiddler's Green someday."

He drained his glass, then poured hers into the ocean. Jack picked up the box and checked the twine to make sure it was secure. Hesitantly, he gently dropped the box over the edge and watched it sink as the boat kept sailing forward.

"Goodbye, my sweet love - I will always miss you."

# VII

Allie's cell phone rang and startled her. She had been sitting silently on her boat, having called off for her shift at the pub. She read the name on the caller ID. Jack - Sat Phone. Her stomach sank as she answered. If he was on his sat phone, he was offshore. If he was offshore, he may not be coming back. She had tried to steady herself for this moment, but nothing she had done prepared her for the feeling she now experienced as she answered the phone, "Jack, are you OK? Where are you?"

He sensed her tension and realized what he had put her through, "I'm fine, I'm about eight miles offshore."

"Are you coming back?" she choked as she said the words.

"I just tacked, and I'm headed back in. I won't be sailing anywhere without you, Allie."

Finally, she felt a sense of relief. She breathed in deeply and exhaled slowly.

"Can you meet me at my slip in two hours?" Jack asked.

"Yeah."

"I have some things I want to tell you. Thanks Allie."

# VIII

Allie was standing at the dock when *Windborne* made the turn into the slip. She picked up the spring line and tossed its spliced end over the cleat on the middle of the yacht, before walking back and handing the stern line to Jack.

"The lines were on the dock," she said to him.

"Huh?"

"You didn't take the lines. If I'd walked over here, I could have seen that you left the lines - that you were coming back."

"Oh my god, did you think I wasn't coming back?"

He couldn't get off the boat fast enough to put his arms around her.

"I didn't know what to think. You were just gone."

"I'm so sorry. This has been so unfair to you."

"Promise me you won't ever do that to me again, Jack Kelly." Allie shed a few tears of relief. The range of emotion in the last few days had been unbearable. First her dad, then Jack, then the suicide.

"Never again," he said to her, and hugged her tightly. Then he added, "I love you so much."

"I love you, too."

He kept his arms around her, and they stood quietly for a few minutes, listening to the gulls and the ringing of halyards on masts.

"I feel like I haven't eaten in days - any chance you want to go eat?" Jack asked.

"Yeah - I could eat."

"Let's take my dinghy and tie up at the West End Yacht Club. I want to show you something first."

He led her down into the saloon where she saw the picture of Jack and Jen on the table, and the two empty glasses in the sink. She picked up the picture and said, "This is a really nice picture of the two of you - we should frame it."

"You would do that?"

"She's part of who you are, Jack. I'm not in competition with her."

Jack smiled at Allie, and she asked, "Do you want me to put it away in the box?"

"That might be kinda hard, Allie."

"Why?"

It's about five-hundred feet below the surface of the Pacific." He pointed to the southwest, "About eight miles that way."

She looked shocked. It was hard for her to believe that something so deeply personal had been cast off from his life.

"Why?"

"It was time - past time. She would have wanted me to live, to be happy... To be with someone like you."

Allie looked up at him.

"That picture is for me. To remember the good times, to celebrate her life."

"I don't know what to say," Allie said somewhat sheepishly.

"It's alright, nothing more needs to be said."

They climbed up the ladder, out of the cockpit, and down onto the docks, walking to the end of the slip finger where the dinghy was tied off. She held the dinghy firmly against the dock while he stepped in. The outboard started on the first pull.

"Well, that's a miracle," he said as he pointed to the engine. "Never goes on the first pull."

"Maybe the universe knows you need a break," Allie said.

"That would be nice," said the captain.

He pulled away from the dock and made the short trip across La Playa anchorage to the yacht club's dinghy dock.

"They have a pretty good club sandwich," Jack said as they approached the dock where they tied off and got out.

As they walked along the dock, an old male sea lion swam up to see if they had anything of interest. He popped his head out of the water in an upright position and snorted out air. They looked over at him as he stared back at them, then he disappeared under the water.

"That was Jeff," said Jack.

"Jeff?"

"Yeah, that's his name."

"You can recognize sea lions?"

"He's not hard to miss - didn't you see that green fishing lure in the side of his face?"

"No - that's awful. I hope it doesn't hurt him," she said.

They walked arm in arm up the steep gangway to the club. There was an old section of a ship's cutwater that hung above the door frame, and the sign read, *Admiral's Club*. Jack pulled open the heavy wooden door accessorized with a brass porthole window which had long ago adorned a big ship. They were warmly greeted by the hostess, who knew both of them.

"To what do we owe the honor?"

"Desperately in need of a club sando, Chloe," Jack answered.

"A man who knows what he wants - lucky you, Allie." She winked at her.

"Yeah, but that club sandwich is also all he aspires to in life," Allie quipped.

Chloe smiled, "I've done worse sweetie."

She walked them to their table overlooking the water and marina. As she seated them, she asked, "Did you guys hear what happened at the Big Game Club today?"

Jack started to answer, but Allie broke in, "Do you still have those crab cakes? I love them. Can you bring them out first? And two Cokes. Thanks, we are starving."

Chloe knew her well enough to understand that Allie's questions meant, move along and I'll tell you later.

"I'll get that up right away," Chloe said as she pushed her pencil behind her ear.

They both stared out the large glass window at the boats in the marina.

"Thanks for that artful interruption to Chloe's question. At this point, I really don't give a fuck who knows, I just don't want to be the one to tell them."

Allie nodded and looked back out the window.

"It was the same way in Norfolk after the trial. There was a huge article in the local paper that headlined SLEEPING CAPTAIN FOUND GUILTY! - I guess that's what I have to look forward to here. Maybe this time it will be 'Sleeping Captain Extends his Reign of Death.'"

The entire club turned at the booming voice of Ted announcing his arrival. "I'm heeere!" The crowd enthusiastically shouted back, "Ted!"

Next, Bradley, who had walked in next to Ted, uncharacteristically shouted, "Hey, what am I? Chopped fish guts?"

The regulars laughed and started the shouts of "Bradley!" The two men made their way over to the table and slid into the booth without an invitation.

Jack said sarcastically, "Would you boys like to join us?"

Ted responded immediately, "Already did!" And then his laugh echoed through the building, bringing a few more cries of "Ted" from the other patrons.

Chloe reappeared with the drinks and pulled out her pad for Bradley and Ted, neither of whom needed a menu. Bradley went first, "Fish tacos and iced tea in a to-go cup."

"Ditto," echoed Ted.

The table got uncomfortably silent after the server had left. Ted decided to break the ice.

"What happened over there sucks, Jack - but you didn't kill that guy."

Allie was shocked at the direct line Ted had taken. There was a brief silence before Jack responded, "No, I didn't kill him, I killed his sister."

Bradley spoke up next, "The ocean killed her, Jack - not you - and it could have been any one of us at this table in your position."

Ted nodded, "Yeah, man."

"I can't do this captain gig anymore, guys."

"That's fucking bullshit," Ted said.

Allie again was shocked and looked at Jack's face for a reaction. She was also surprised that Bradley didn't step in to mediate as Ted thundered on.

"We all fuck things up bro, that's life. If you don't like it, I think that dude's rope is still on that fish scale. Just check-out if you can't handle it, but for God's sake, stop being a mopey pussy. I mean, we all love you, but enough is enough."

At that, neither Jack, Bradley nor Allie knew what to say. Jack started to shake his head, and then to Bradley and Allie's surprise, he began to laugh softly, saying, "Jesus, Ted, could you be a little more direct? I'm not sure I understand your meaning."

They all laughed tensely.

"You're a captain, Jack, and a damned good one. I'd sail under you any day," Ted said, as he hit his own chest with a closed fist.

"Me too," Bradley offered gently.

"Count me in," Allie said as she squeezed his hand.

Chloe reappeared with Bradley and Ted's drinks, and they sat quietly for a few minutes, checking their phones, looking around at the ceiling filled with club racing pennants, and staring out at the marina.

The food was laid in front of them by one of the other servers. "Chloe's on a short break, just holler if you need anything."

The four of them turned their attention to the food and the topics of discussion took a sudden shift to the comfort of the mundane: did that one asshole tip you? how many phone numbers did you get? I need some help with one of the sail slugs, when are we shifting to the later sunset sail?

Then, toward the end of their meal, Allie broke into the captain chatter.

"Jack, you never told me what happened after you left Norfolk."

"Oh boy, here we go," said Bradley, who knew the whole story.

"Oh, this sounds juicy!" Ted said as he leaned in.

Bradley shook his head from side to side and waved his hands back and forth while he smiled and said,

"I think we've learned enough about Captain Jack today, let's save that story for a rum-soaked night. Right now, we've got boats to sail."

## Acknowledgements

- ❖ My thanks to Jim and Lisa for giving a very rough first draft a read and providing input

- ❖ My thanks to NOAA for checking my notes on weather

- ❖ My thanks to Captain Mel Stackpoole, owner of Great Lakes Charter Training (GLC Training), for confirming those many details that are too numerous to remember

- ❖ My thanks to Sail San Diego and its captains, for their continued friendship and support – take a sail with them if you are ever in San Diego

- ❖ My thanks to my Senior Editor and Developmental Editor, Morgan and Dave Bone for your advice and support

- ❖ My thanks to Laury Falter (The Guardian Saga), for your continued belief in my writing

- ❖ My thanks to Chris Durbin (Carlisle and Holbrooke Naval Adventures) for your advice and wisdom

- ❖ My never-ending thanks to my wife Laurie – without you, none of this would have been possible

- ❖ With the deepest gratitude, my thanks to the United States Coast Guard, who always answers the call.

## About Marine Life & The Ocean

Do whales really get entangled and rescued? The short answer is yes. For further reading, NOAA Fisheries published a report titled, 2021 West Coast Entanglement Summary. YouTube also has a number of videos that show boaters helping marine mammals, including whales. It's amazing, or perhaps we shouldn't be surprised, but the mammals always seem grateful to those that have helped them. Perhaps we are not as far removed from these distant branches of the genetic tree as we may think. If you need a what's in it for me? Just remember, we depend on the ocean for food, and maintaining our weather, let's take care of it.

As an ocean crossing sailor, I have seen some awful sights, like trash fifteen-hundred-miles offshore. I have seen sea lions with fishing lures stuck in their face (Just like 'Jeff' in the book). Our species is having an adverse effect on the oceans, and we have to all work together to undo some of the damage. Please consider challenging yourself to reduce your plastic usage. Choose glass, metal, aluminum, or cardboard containers when possible. Write letters to your favorite food company. Even small steps are action in the right direction.

# Thank <u>You</u> – The Reader!

I sincerely appreciate you reading *The Captain – Point Loma*. This is the first book in what is planned to be a series. If you enjoyed reading *The Captain*, please consider leaving a review on Amazon or Goodreads, as well as sharing on social media.

If you would like to learn more about how I became a captain and author, please consider my memoir **Two Years Behind the Helm**, which is available on Amazon.

My email address is <u>camseamus@outlook.com</u> if you would like to drop me a note or be added to my mailing list for future book releases.

## About the Author

Cam Séamus grew up in Dana Point, and spent much of his youth in, on, and around the water. He learned to sail at a U.S. Navy recreational program while serving in the United Sates Marine Corps. He is an American Sailing Association Instructor, and Master, Near Coastal (Captain). He has worked as an instructor, sailboat charter captain, and delivery captain. He holds a B.S. in Marketing from Grand Canyon University.

Cam is currently working on several projects, including the prequel to The Captain. He enjoys spending time with his wife and their dogs in Southern California and enjoys sailing all over the world.

## Basic Sailing Terms

AIS – an electronic signal and receiver showing where boats are and showing others your position

Berth – a place to sleep, or a place to dock the boat

Boom – horizontal pole that holds the bottom of the sail

Bow – front

Cockpit – the area where there are usually seats and the helm

Chines – a pronounced change in the angle of the boats hull as it comes up to the topsides – this can be a visible line seen along the waterline

Dock Line – used to secure the boat to the dock

Galley – the kitchen

GPS – Global positioning system; satellites that identify your position on the earth

Halyard – for hauling up the sail

Head – the bathroom

Heave-To (Hove-To) – Heaving-to is a technique that balances the wind, sails, and helm, essentially "parking" the boat, allowing it to drift with the wind and current

Helm or Wheel – the device used to steer the boat

Hull – the part of the boat that is in and above the water

In Irons – when the bow of a sailboat is pointed directly into the wind, or inside of the "no sail zone" there is no lift being created by the sail and the sails flap

Jacklines – web lines that are affixed to the bow and stern of each side of the boat. These are attachment points for the harness lanyard when in stormy weather.

Keel – a "fin" on the bottom of the boat that keeps it from slipping sideways and provides stability. They come in a variety of shapes, sizes, and attachment types.

Lifelines – normally cable line that goes around the edges of the boat, held in place by stations

Lines – anything that you would call 'rope' on land, is a line on a sailboat, the names change with its job

Mast – upright vertical pole that holds the sail

No Sail Zone – sailboats cannot sail directly into the wind, or within about forty-five degrees to either side of the direction of the wind. These ninety degrees make up the No Sail Zone

On The Hard – a term used for boats that are out of the water on supports, generally at a boat yard for repairs

Port – left

Prop Walk – the effect a propeller can have on a boat in reverse, moving it to one side or the other depending on the direction the blade is turning

Reefing – taking in sail during heavy weather

Rounding Up – when a sailboat becomes over-powered (too much wind and sail), it will turn itself into the wind as a safety mechanism to reduce knockdowns

Saloon – the area below decks where there is usually a dining and seating area

Sheet – controls sail angle (in and out)

Shrouds – wires that hold the mast in place

Slip – a place to dock the boat

Starboard – right

Stern – rear

Topsides – the part of the hull that is above the waterline – between the waterline and the deck

Weather Decks – the deck area ahead of the cockpit


This is a non-exhaustive list designed to help the reader understand nautical terms. If you are interested in learning more, I recommend that you find an American Sailing Association school and take ASA 101.